THE
PROMISE ROSE

THE
PROMISE ROSE

•

Joan Vincent

AVALON BOOKS
NEW YORK

PRINTED IN THE UNITED STATES OF AMERICA
ON ACID-FREE PAPER
BY HADDON CRAFTSMEN, BLOOMSBURG, PENNSYLVANIA

To
Old Friends of many years
To
Vera, who believed and encouraged
To
New Friends and what is yet to come

Prologue—1748

The two young ladies on the garden path walked as closely together as the wide hip hoops beneath their Watteau-style gowns permitted. Their huge sleeve bows danced a minuet to their whispered confidences. Near a small pool at the end of the garden they rested upon a stone bench, shaded from the afternoon sun by a huge beech tree, ancient as the estate upon which it stood.

"Oh, Glenna," Barry said as one of her friend's burnished gold curls sprang from its pin and bobbed free beneath the delicate lace morning cap. She refastened the lock, then carefully ran a hand over her own dark brown hair, meticulously dressed in close, tight curls.

"What is it, a loose curl?" Glenna said, her bright blue eyes sparkling. "Must you be so very serious about everything?" she said to her friend. "Mr. Mc-Dowell is not so grim." She paused, and then clapped her hands in delight. "If he and I happen to be alone this evening, I must contrive for a curl to fall free so he can pin it for me."

"You would not!" gasped Barry. She blushed fiercely.

1

"Why he—he could take advantage of the moment and—and kiss you!"

"Oh, I do hope so," Glenna said, sighing. "Barry, you needn't look so shocked—he and I are to be wed."

Both young ladies giggled nervously.

Glenna studied her companion curiously. "Have you truly never been kissed?"

"You know I have not been in society as much as you," Barry said, her brown eyes darkening in reflection. "Father does not often call me home from school. I do thank you for having me come home with you so often."

"After you saved me from that horrid Mrs. Mumpkin?" Glenna asked. "Such a nasty scolding and all over a little mouse. How was I to know she would take such a fright? I could do no less for you. We shall always be friends. When Mr. McDowell and I are wed you shall come often to visit."

"Do you 'care' for him?" Barry asked.

"I suppose I must, since we are to be wed. Mother says it does not matter. She insists marriage is so much more agreeable when one's affections are not involved," Glenna said. "But let us speak of you. What of Prideau?" She watched Barry's cheeks turn a soft rose red. "Ah, you do care for him then. You must allow him to walk with you in the gardens this evening."

"I do not think he is interested in that way. He only likes to discuss Mr. Pelham's programs with me and speak of his work. He intends to enter the Commons." Barry raised her eyes from the pool's glossy surface.

"I cannot believe that is all," Glenna assured her. "He watches you whenever he thinks no one may notice it." She shrugged. "Prideau would be far too serious for me. But, well, you seem well matched. I shall speak—"

"Oh, Glenna!" Barry protested, taking her hand. "You would not, could not be so forward. I could never forgive you. There is not hope that such as I can attract Prideau."

"Melloncourt," Glenna replied. She laughed gaily at Barry's consternation. "Lady Melloncourt. Don't you remember? The scandal two years ago. Well, there were those who said she had no looks and no dowry, but still she wed a duke. You are vastly more handsome." Glenna took in Barry's statuesque height, the clear, rose-petal complexion and luxurious chestnut curls. "If only you did not persist in being such a bluestocking. Mrs. Montague might be pleased to hear that you read such things as Swift and Pope, and that you speak of their work with understanding, but really, Barry, that is what deters any man from approaching you. You know I have not a single feather to fly with for a brain and I am to be wed to Mr. McDowell."

Barry rose to continue their walk, saying nothing. The truth of Glenna's words was well-verified by her lack of suitors. Even had there been many, she was wise enough to know that as the daughter of a minor gentry family of merely adequate means her chances of a "good" match were small. But Prideau had shown a lack of concern for such matters and hope had tenaciously woven a tentacle about her heart.

Barry released a soft, lengthy sigh as she watched the graceful curtsies of a rainbow of satin and silk gowns in the movements of the stately minuet. She had escaped Glenna's latest effort, the elderly Lord Gromley, a widower from the Cotswolds who had brightened visibly when introduced to the young but serious-minded miss.

It was very warm in the ballroom, and Barry fanned her face, wishing she had not consented to wear the heavy satin gown Glenna had brought to her chamber that afternoon. Glancing down at the much-furbelowed golden skirt draped over the wide whalebone hoop, however, she smiled. It was an exquisite gown and she did feel beautiful. *If only it were not the elderly gentlemen who noted it,* she thought. Her eyes flickered across the company of dancers, seeking a tall, thin gentleman with a quiet, subdued presence.

At the sound of a voice at her side, Barry started; then, seeing it was Prideau, smiled. "Yes?"

"It is quite warm, what with the candles and the great crowd. That is, I was wondering if you might wish a walk in the gardens." He hurried his words, suddenly nervous. "Near the lantern light, of course," he added hastily when she hesitated.

"Why, yes. That would be pleasant." Barry took his arm, a tremor running through her under his warm smile, the gentle appeal of his dark eyes.

They walked silently for a pace, moving away from the other strollers. Barry glanced at him and wondered at his lack of words, for they usually conversed freely.

"May I ask you a question of a most personal nature?" Prideau said suddenly.

His simple earnestness struck her heart a fatal blow. "If you wish."

"Has anyone—has your father been approached—that is, are you promised in marriage?" His firm lips tightened, bracing for the reply.

Barry's cheeks paled. "No," she said, her heart hammering in her ears.

"I see," he said with a sigh of relief, then pressed

her to walk forward, taking the time to choose his words carefully as they moved beyond the veranda. "I am but two and twenty, far too young to wed," Prideau told her. "But I believe the selection of one's lifelong companion to be a most serious matter. Do you believe arranged marriages, such as that of Miss Adden and Mr. McDowell, are for the best?"

"I—I had not thought on it," she replied, trying to understand his meaning. "It is the usual manner of betrothal and both seem pleased."

"But is the mutual enhancement of families, and their security, the only goal of marriage?" His eyes darkened, his somber demeanor intensified.

Barry frowned. She struggled to defend Glenna's choice and yet answer honestly.

"I mean no insult to your friend," Prideau said to her. "But to my thinking, happiness in one's choice of wife or husband should never rest on an assessment of his or her worldly possessions."

Prideau gazed at the tall beauty, bathed in the pale moonlight. The young man drew a deep breath. "I am but a second son and, as such, have little to offer. In a month I must go to visit my father's lands in the American colonies. I may be gone for some time, a year, perhaps even longer. But while there, I hope to advance myself." An intense hope shone in his eyes. He took her hands in his. "Do I dare too much to hope that—could we not exchange letters during this time?"

She had not dared to hope that he cared for her. "It would be an honor," Barry said.

"If I can manage it, I shall visit your home before I go. I would not want your father to think ill of my forwardness in speaking to you."

"I am certain he shall not, but it would not matter,"

she replied, the knowledge of his feelings embolden-
ing her.

The stubborn rise of her chin brought a smile to his
lips. "May I use your given name?"

Barry leaned forward to catch the softly spoken
words. Her closeness proved too much for the young
man's resolution. His arms slipped about her, his lips
closed gently on hers. They parted slowly, gazing in
wonder at each other. After a long moment, Prideau
spoke. "This shall be our pledge. It shall not be broken
by time or distance," he said.

"As you say it," Barry said, wishing to laugh and
cry at the same time, for she saw all he wished to say
in his eyes even as he read the same in hers.

Raising her hand to his lips, he kissed it lightly, then
drew her to him. "I have never said this to anyone
before. I love you."

"And I—I love you," she answered shyly, raising
her face to receive his kiss.

Moments later Prideau reluctantly pulled back, his
gaze lingering on her face, then he turned, placed her
hand upon his arm and glanced about. "We must return to the ballroom," he said regretfully.

On the veranda elderly Lord Gromley stood frowning into the dimly lit night. He watched the young
couple slowly returning, an aura of happiness sur-
rounding them as it had not done before. He resolved
to act at once.

"Barry! Barry? Why are you hiding here?" Glenna
asked, entering an arbor she and her friend frequented.
"Mother's seamstress wishes to give your gown for
the wedding a fitting." She paused. "Have you—are
you crying?" Glenna hurried to her.

Barry wiped away her tears with her kerchief and stood. "It is—nothing." An object fell from the folds of her skirt.

"What a beautiful rose," Glenna said, retrieving it. "A red rose, *la rose d'amour.*" She arched a brow teasingly. "Prideau?" A squeal of delight escaped at Barry's nod. "Oh, do tell me what has happened."

"Four days ago—the night of the ball, we went for a walk in the garden. He asked if we might exchange missives while he is in America," Barry reluctantly told her. Her color rose. "He repeated his request when you left us alone at the picnic yesterday."

"Is he to call on your father before he leaves?"

"He spoke of visiting my home but we did not speak of marriage—not directly. There has been so little time." Barry blinked back tears, reached out, and gently took the rose from Glenna's hand, cradling it tenderly.

"A walk in the garden," Barry said. "A magic moment during a picnic. And now there is no time." Her face began to crumble. "He has been summoned home—he departed this morning." A tear fell onto the fragile rose petals. "A maid brought this to me," she caressed the rose, "with a note that he would come the next time I was given such a rose. That he would then be free to speak its—message."

Glenna blinked several times then beamed. "Oh, my. I never would have believed it of Prideau."

"I can hardly credit that he loves me."

Seeing the wonder shine in Barry's eyes, her deep vulnerability, Glenna wished to caution her. "You must remember that men are rather strange creatures. Mother says they often say things they do not mean—and that is true. Two months ago Mr. Retrand was swearing his undying devotion to me and now he is betrothed to another."

"But Prideau did mean it," Barry replied vehemently. "My heart will break if he did not. It will."

Chapter One

London 1760

The cold wind in the London street cleared the haze from Barry's mind. Anger at the petty nastiness of her dead husband's barrister was only one emotion clamoring among many. The estate was far deeper in debt than she could imagine. *How am I to save the estate for my stepson, Patrick, and his sister Pamela?* Barry thought.

An unruly team in the street reared and lashed out at their traces. The angry driver whipped them down, causing one to neigh in anger and pain.

A squall of snow swept past and instead of the carriage Barry saw huntsmen racing through the Cotswold countryside, her portly husband in the lead. Then the hedge, the higher stone wall behind it. She heard the snap of bone as his hunter failed to make the jump. Its shrill cry as it went down. Then her husband, lying on the ground, unreasonably still, confusion reigning all about.

The carriage moved on; the scene vanished as quickly as it had appeared, but not the dread it evoked.

Death—so precipitate, so perturbing, so permanent. Once again it had taken all and left her to manage with only her pride.

The shops along Queen Street went unnoticed as scenes from her past parleyed with the future. *Has it only been five years since Father died?* she asked herself. Then, like now, she had faced a barrister who had spoken the sinister words "debts" and "sale," but at least he had been kind.

Did this new barrister's malice spring from believing she had married Gromley only for his money?

Well, Barry thought, *isn't he correct?*

What choice did you have? An inner voice asked bitterly. The panic, the horrible indecision of those days came back with crushing force.

Six years before her father's death she had refused her only marriage proposal and had never encouraged like-minded men. With his demise she faced penury, and there was but one moral means of survival. For three years Barry had had her pride daily buffeted and bruised by the niggling demands of an aged cousin who never failed to remind her of the gratitude owed.

A chance encounter with the elderly Lord Gromley, her rejected suitor, had renewed his interest. Barry no longer found him the elderly, gouty nuisance of her naïve youth. The drudgery of her days had transformed him into a gentleman who carried his sixty years well. His renewed offer of marriage brought on a practical and painfully realistic assessment of her future. She had reluctantly consented.

Gromley had proven no worse than most husbands. Barry alone knew the price she paid for surrendering her dreams. Hiding her bruised spirit, she learned to take joy in her home. Her young stepson attempted to make her welcome which cushioned his sister's continuing resentment.

Barry shook herself from her reverie. *Whatever am I to do?* Her eyes clouded with tears. She bumped into a man who bobbed his head, a leering smile on his lips.

Gathering her skirts, Barry ran forward heedlessly. Her hurried steps carried her towards the river. She did not falter even when splashed with mud and water by passing coaches in the evening twilight. Only when winded by her run did Barry slow her steps.

She blinked back half-frozen tears of despair. Before her stood the new Westminster Bridge, the Thames River blending with the sky in the deepening dusk. Walking slowly across it, she halted near its center. Chunks of ice danced amidst the flotsam in the river below, beckoning her while the icy wind whispered its deadly promises. She clutched the stone edge. Anxiety, pain, betrayal, skittered in her mind like water wraiths.

Why go on? Why? The children—

Unheard, a bell-like voice ordered a stylish landau to halt near Barry. Bright blue eyes peered at her from the window.

What will you do? Barry demanded of herself. *Patrick needs me—trusts me.* A great sob escaped her. If only there was someone to turn to—someone she could trust.

Barry jerked away when a hand gingerly touched her shoulder. Her eyes widened in disbelief at the sight of the diminutive form before her—a vision from her past.

Pushing back the white ermine-edged hood of her cloak, Glenna McDowell shook her burnished curls. "Barry, how delightful to see you!"

Barry's knees grew suddenly weak and she fell to the street in a dead faint.

Barry fumbled to push the pungent hartshorne away.

"That is better," a soft voice said happily. "Drink this." A cup pressed against her lips.

A fiery liquid burned a path down Barry's throat. She spluttered, forced her eyes open, and attempted to rise.

"I do think you had best remain lying down for a time," Glenna said to her old friend.

Surrendering to the surprisingly strong pressure of the dainty hands against her shoulders, Barry relaxed against the pillows of the settee and struggled for a coherent thought.

"Much better," Glenna said with a smile. "I have ordered some broth for you. That will help dispel the chill."

Chill. The word sent icy needles stabbing through Barry's hands and feet. *How long had I walked in the bitter cold? Where am I?* Her eyes ran over the sumptuous room with its silk damask drapery, velvet-covered furniture, and roaring fire. "Where are we?" she managed to say at last.

"At my town house in Hanover Square. Oh, Tabu, bring the broth here." She turned to the small figure who was silently entering the chamber.

Barry's eyes widened at the sight of the small, young African, a red and yellow striped turban atop his head and a red suit snugly fitting his sturdy form.

"I'll take it, Tabu." Glenna reached for the bowl and spoon on the silver tray he carried. She daintily placed a spoonful of broth in her friend's gaping mouth. "Now swallow." She laughed, dismissing the page with a nod. Continuing the spoonfuls as rapidly as

Barry could swallow, she said, "When we have you properly warmed you will tell me how I came to find you on Westminster Bridge." Her tone was light but concern clouded her features.

Only after dutifully finishing the last ounce was Barry permitted to speak. "I was walking—I forgot where I was going," she said. Then cocking a wary brow, she studied Glenna. "How did you know it was I?"

"It has been many years, has it not? Twelve since I was wed. Six since our last letters crossed paths if I recollect correctly," she said, a hint of guilt lacing her voice.

"Do not fret," Barry assured her. "It was as much my neglect as yours. We just—changed. Drifted into different worlds." She shrugged. "You still have not said how you knew it was I."

"For that." Glenna waved a hand negligently. "It was your walk. You need not look so disbelieving. I saw this figure from my carriage who reminded me of my dear friend Barry," she said soothingly, seeing the other's dismay. "What is wrong?"

Barry sought to distract her. "Mr. McDowell? Is he at home?"

"In Scotland as he wished." A shadow flitted across Glenna's features. "He died three years past."

"Were you happy?"

Glenna forced a laugh. "What an odd question." Barry's interest prodded her to continue. "He was a dear, kind man. I mourned his passing until I realized he meant me to continue as before. You can see," she motioned to the chamber's furnishings, "he left me comfortably settled. Yes, Mr. McDowell was a good kind man." She smiled at pleasant memories before returning to her original question. "But what of you all these years?"

"There is not much to tell." Barry shrugged, looking from Glenna to the fire. "Father died five years ago and my husband last year."

"You *did* marry then?" Her surprise showed. "I thought—"

Barry hastened to interrupt her. "Lord Gromley was my husband. We were wed three years past."

"He offered for you a second time?" Glenna studied the other closely. "I had heard he had wed someone less than half his age but had no idea—"

"There was no reason for you to surmise it was I. We had a quiet wedding at my cousin's home."

"And was your marriage happy?"

Barry looked away. "It was not unhappy. My stepson, Patrick is a joy." She frowned. "His sister Pamela drives me to distraction at times and when she learns—" she halted, felt a blush creep up her face.

"What is it, Barry?" Glenna said gently. "You know you can trust me."

"I do need to tell someone," Barry said and blurted out her recent discovery of Gromley's many gambling debts. "I have come to London to see what could be done," she said.

"Then you shall stay with me while you get matters settled." Glenna paused. "And your stepchildren also."

"Thank you," Barry said, relief that one problem was solved. "But Pamela, my stepdaughter, is staying with an aunt and Patrick is at school. They are not to return to Gromley Hall until I write when I am to return."

"Then you are my guest," Glenna said adamantly. She looked at Barry tentatively. "There was a rumor after Gromley's death that his widow was to remarry.

Do not glare at me so. England is full of women forced
to starve, become mistresses, or remarry. Even I was
traded for a parcel of land," she said, laughing too
brightly.

Reaching for Glenna's hand and giving it a squeeze,
Barry said, "I am not to remarry. And I am very tired.
Can you see to a chair for me? I must return to the
White Swan and fetch my bandbox before they sell it
for the inn's fee."

"I will send my footman at once to take care of both
matters." Glenna rose. "We have much to chat about.
London was beginning to be dreadfully dull." She
halted before the gilded double doors of the chamber.
"Rest. I shall return soon," she said and slipped
through them.

Barry snuggled deeper beneath the coverlets and
sighed. It would be a relief not to worry, even for a
short time. She looked about the large chamber.

A chill deeper than any caused by winter's icy
winds ran through her at sight of a vase on the sideboard. She closed her eyes with a mental curse against
her weakness. After all these years, the sight of a
blood-red rose, of this one innocently posing on the
sideboard, should not cause such deep pain.

"You must learn not to stare so," Glenna McDowell
admonished Barry early one morning during the first
week of her stay. "One would think you had never
seen a page."

"In truth, I have seen very few." Barry took her gaze
from the small, sturdy figure of Tabu, who had remained impervious to her inspection.

"You worry too much about others, Barry. It always
was your worst failing," Glenna told her. "He is not
unhappy.

"From what you have told me there is but one person you should be concerned about at the moment. There, I have made you frown," she said. "And that will never do.

"Tabu, see that my coach is brought to the door. We must be off to do our shopping. It is only three days before the ball," she reminded Barry.

"I cannot part with even a guinea until I—"

"Don't worry. I know the most reasonable seamstresses." She winked. "One gown will do no harm and a vast amount of good. Come." Her eyes twinkled an impish appeal.

The years rolled away swiftly under that gaze. Glenna had not changed in the least. Mischief was still her ally. Certain she would not, Barry said, "If the cost is—reasonable."

"And that gold velvet, Barry. I always said you looked best in gold, especially with that dark mane of yours."

"But I can scarcely breathe," Barry said as the seamstress tugged the last button of the gown over its loop.

"Breathe? My dear, a slim figure is more essential. Breathing? It is—superfluous." She shrugged nonchalantly. "You have but to look in the mirror to see a tight corset is worth the discomfort. All London shall be agog wondering who you are."

Barry heard mischief echoing. "Glenna, none of your plotting." Further words were prevented by the seamstress fastening a golden silk ruffle about her throat.

At her startled expression, Glenna smiled reassuringly. "It is the height of fashion. At least it will be when we find the proper accessories and a peruke. Or do you prefer to powder your own hair? Never mind.

"We shall take the gown," she said to the beaming seamstress, who seemed far too accustomed to her friend's ways for Barry's comfort. "And the hoops and petticoats, of course. Send it all to my house by to-morrow."

The small wave of purchases began to swell, and swept Barry along as the morning progressed. Returning to 21 Hanover Square with barely a corner of the coach left for them, she was certain they were about to drown her.

"Please see that these boxes are placed in Lady Gromley's chambers," Glenna said to her stolid butler as Tabu and the footmen struggled beneath the mound of bandboxes. "And have tea brought to the salon.

"Come along, Barry. There is much we must discuss."

"I most certainly agree," Barry answered vehemently.

Glenna judged the moment ripe for silence. With delaying ceremony she carefully sat and straightened the ruching on her embroidered stomacher while her friend paced before her.

Clenching her hands, Barry halted before her. "Every last purchase must be sent back," she said. "I know you mean to pay for them and I cannot consent to it."

"My dear Barry, you have been in the country too long. One never pays a bill at the time of purchase. It would be too—common. No, in London a dun is sent after a reasonable period to assure that one is satisfied. You would insult the shopkeepers by doing it differently.

"The bills will be given to you the moment they

arrive. I will swear by Prime Minister Pitt's oath," she said.

The guileless look did not reassure Barry, but she knew not how to combat the sensible argument. "But they must be far too expensive for me," she started to say.

"Nonsense. The whole sum cannot be more than a mere—£5," Glenna's voice rose hopefully at naming the amount, warning Barry it was far too little.

"Truly?" she said.

"Barry, do you not remember our childhood? Did I ever lead you astray or tell you a falsehood?" Her seriousness faltered. "Never mind answering that," she said with a laugh. "We have far more serious matters to attend.

"When was the last time you danced? Do you know a gavotte from a gigue?" She hopped up and grabbed Barry's hand. "It would be a sure wager you do not." She wagged a finger accusingly. "You must recall the minuet, though. It has not altered that much since you last danced." The corners of Glenna's mouth twitched into a half frown. "We shall begin lessons at once."

"But," Barry objected hesitantly, puzzling at her friend's near-hypnotic hold.

"Well?" Glenna tapped her foot impatiently.

The reasons for objecting to attending the ball that had been teeming in her mind just moments before escaped Barry. A reluctant smile curved her lips. It was clear Glenna was determined and it was not likely that even the Almighty could sway her.

"Oh, Glenna." Barry laughed freely for the first time in months. She feigned horror. "Of course I cannot disgrace you by mistaking a musette for a gigue. How appalling that would be."

Glenna's laughter belled lightly. *Ah*, she thought,

breathing an inner sigh of relief, *much of the old Barry is still there. It will need but a little coaxing to lure her back to her former nature.* A smile hid the thought. "I am so relieved you see what is important."

Chapter Two

The butler's sonorous voice announced the ladies' entry into the Bordon ballroom. "Lady Gromley and Mrs. McDowell."

A tug at Barry's sleeve interrupted her fascinated gaping at the monstrous wigs, some over three feet in height, worn by some of the guests.

"You must not stare," Glenna scolded behind her fluttering fan. "Ah, here is Lord John Halsey." She dropped into a low curtsy, which Barry imitated.

Glenna tossed a smile at her host and drew Barry forward. "He has never wed and is a fine figure of a man for his three and forty years," she whispered.

"Now Glenna," Barry warned.

"I did not mean for you to take an interest," she said in mock surprise. "I have been a widow far longer than you."

"Oh," Barry's voice trailed to embarrassed silence, her guard momentarily lowered.

Introductions were made to several other distinguished gentlemen. Barry danced often. Allowed to rejoin Glenna after several dances, she gratefully accepted the champagne Lord John offered. At Glenna's prompting, she allowed him to claim her for an assembling minuet. When he led her from the floor, they were halted by a tall, handsome figure in red silk who made a leg—bowing while extending the leg as was customary—before Barry.

"May I have the pleasure of leading you in the allemande?" the gentleman asked smoothly.

Barry looked to Lord John, thinking he knew the gentleman.

He, believing she knew the man, graciously agreed.

The various steps of the allemande permitted her to surreptitiously inspect her partner. She approved the modest tallwig above the overlong face. The fine line of his cheekbones was his best feature, contrasting with smallish eyes. His shoulders were wide, their line firm above a pair of finely turned calves and a trim waist. She put aside a sense of distaste that crept over her when she happened to catch him studying her much as a hunter studies his partridges.

"You are a most graceful dancer, Lady Gromley." The thin lips curved into a suave smile as the strains of the violins faded.

"I fear you have me at a disadvantage, sir," she returned, pleasantly surprised to find such prattle come so easily.

"I am Looten, my lady." He made a flourish with his hand. "Alfred Looten, Esquire."

"Have you known Mrs. McDowell long?" Barry asked when he said no more.

"She is a charming woman," he answered smoothly. "But I am most delighted to find you in London." Looten took two goblets of champagne from a passing footman and handed one to Barry. "I myself am only recently returned from the Continent. It was my intent to call at Gromley Hall later this month."

"Then you knew my husband?" she asked.

"Yes." He paused and smiled, a hint of teasing accusation in his eyes. "You do recall that we are neighbors? But then I have not been to Looten's Loft for several years," he added cajolingly.

Balancing flattery with questions, Looten guided Barry back towards Glenna.

But oddly, she found herself a little relieved when he excused himself and disappeared into the throng.

"Do come," Glenna called out gaily, the tip of her fan bobbing above the heads of her beaux. "That was a handsome gentleman," she whispered in an aside when Barry joined her. Her fan poised dramatically. "These gentlemen wish us to attend a masque at Raneleagh tomorrow evening," she said with just enough hesitancy to assure a chorus of pleas from the eager men.

"My lords, good sirs," Glenna said. "My dear friend disapproves of such entertainments."

At once assurances of sobriety, gaiety, and propriety came from the men. All overruled Barry's timid objections. She found herself with the choice of giving her consent or being condemned for ruining the evening for all. Glenna's artless look prompted her to choose the latter, but a plea from Lord John disallowed the intent. Barry went against her judgment once again.

Glenna leaned limply against the velvet cushions in her closed carriage on the return to Hanover Square. "I am exhausted. Wasn't the music delightful? You learned your meager dance lessons well, Barry. The gentlemen were quite taken with you. Even Lord John commented, and he is usually so smitten with me that he notices no one else."

"I cannot credit that he did so," Barry replied. "He was being polite. The only reason I danced was because you refused to do so with any gentleman until he had squired me," she said indignantly.

"How can you imagine such foolishness?" Glenna said.

"It is not as if you had never done it before," Barry scoffed. Her indignation softened. "I know you mean well, Glenna, but please, give me your oath that tomorrow evening at the masque, you will contrive nothing. Absolutely nothing."

"In truth, you do not need such paltry contrivance," Glenna replied calculatingly. "That handsome gentleman who stole you from Lord John is ample proof of that."

"You mean the gentleman in the red silk? Why, I thought he was known to you—No matter, as it happens he is a neighbor to Gromley Hall—Alfred Looten."

"A rare figure of a man," Glenna said. "His looks are hawkish but pleasing, and there is a virility about him which attracts one. It shall be interesting if he should appear at the masque. Your first conquest. Now you are frowning again." She sighed. A moment later Glenna sat up. "I forgot my surprise. Remember how you used to carry on about Lady Mary Montague when we were at school. Was it her Turkey letters?"

"Embassy letters, Glenna," Barry said, failing to stifle a laugh. "Her husband was ambassador to Constantinople."

"Who cares if it be a country or a meal?" Glenna waved her words aside with a flutter of her fan. "I have received permission to call on Lady Montague. You must stay another week," she said triumphantly.

* * *

Nervously contemplating the evening before her, Barry found herself approaching Raneleagh Gardens on the Thames in one of the many watercrafts for hire. Familiar with the celebrated dining parties of Raneleagh from articles in *Gentleman's Magazine*, Barry knew the main entertainment was dining in boxes lining the sides of the huge Rotunda while a mixture of peerage, gentry, and the common curious promenaded about the huge pillared center fireplace to the music of an orchestra set on tiers before a great organ. Glenna had assured her that this evening's masque would be much the same but with the addition of dancing and the concealing dominoes—loose hooded cloaks with half masks.

A burst of laughter from her companions brought Barry's eyes to Glenna's. The dangerous sparkle in her friend's eyes did not foretell the decorous evening promised.

Their boatman took little note of the many crafts vying to land their charges at the river's entrance of the Gardens, but Barry was dismayed at the sight. She wished for a share of his unconcern as she clutched the side of the rocking boat with one hand, held her mask in place with the other.

The boatman nudged the dock and those on it held the boat close. Lord John stepped out and handed Glenna to land. Swallowing the lump in her throat, Barry managed to disembark without tripping. She was conscious of a growing unease that had began with dressing for the masque. The silent plea to return to Hanover Square she threw at Glenna was ignored.

"Come." Lord John gently took Barry's arm and drew her forward, following Glenna up the path leading to the Rotunda.

Dozens of lanterns and torches illuminated the exterior of the great dome, twinkling like an army of fireflies.

"Is it not grand?" Glenna squeezed Barry's hand. "Smile. This is an evening you shall always remember." She reached up and dexterously loosened the cords holding Barry's cloak and expertly retied them to reveal her stunning blue velvet gown. The elaborate silver quilting of its stomacher glittered in the torch and candlelight, enhancing Barry's slender form to perfection.

"Magnifique." Glenna smiled at the results, then straightened her own full skirt of rose-colored silk brocade over hoops before daringly shrugging her domino off her left shoulder.

"If we become separated simply look for the posy." She motioned to the spray of violets on her domino. "I shall know you by this." She pinned a broach just below Barry's right shoulder.

"Lord John, shall we join the promenade?" Glenna motioned Barry to follow.

Entering the vast Rotunda, Barry gazed in wonder at the huge blue dome with its ornate boxes lining the sides. The high gallery for those only able to afford the price to gape at the wonders below was filling. She looked about and drank in the rich silks and brocades of the men and the satins and velvets of the women, all adorned with perukes and periwigs, some outlandishly decorated with fruits, birds, or all manner of flower and vegetation. Sprinkled throughout, she also noticed the less well-dressed, the over and underdressed, and recalled Lord John's frowning statement that all who could afford the crown entry price were allowed entry. Wonder changed to displeasure as two men not far from her began arguing.

Barry looked about for Glenna and was alarmed to

find her friend nowhere in sight. *I couldn't have paused that long*, she thought, exasperated by her carelessness. Annoyance turned to dismay when she found her arm in the clutch of a masked man. He staggered towards the dancers, Barry in his hold.

"Unhand me, sir," she protested, bracing her weight against his steps.

"You are a fine woman," he said, leering at her.

Barry twisted in his hold, her fear rising.

"You have made a mistake, sir."

The deep, chilling voice halted the man. "What, my lord?" He twisted to see who had spoken.

A strong hand freed Barry's wrist. " "My lady, I fear I was delayed over long."

Barry read assurance of her safety in his deep brown eyes.

"My—my pardon, my lord," he said, hastening away.

Dexterously shielding her from another stumbling gentleman, the tall, blue-dominoed rescuer took Barry's arm.

The warmth of his hand, the leap of her pulse at his touch altered fear to confusion. "Thank you for your aid." Barry stared at his hand and then slowly looked up to meet his gaze. She tried to temper her frown of self-recrimination. "It was kind of you to rescue me from—from an unpleasant situation."

"It was my pleasure." He nodded, his demeanor stiffening perceptibly as she spoke. "You are unescorted?"

Barry saw he thought her behavior improper and felt a blush rise. "No, I am with friends. We somehow became separated."

"Then may I have the pleasure of this dance?" He made a gracious bow. "It will make it easier to move through the crowd and perhaps we shall spy your friends as we dance."

She wrenched her eyes from his, and spoke more sharply than she intended. "I hope so."

Her gallant took her hand, his smile tempered into a quizzical turn.

Walking with him, Barry was acutely conscious of her tall rescuer. His blue domino did not conceal his form, neither too paltry nor too plump but of solid trimness. Dark brows told of dark hair beneath the simple bagwig. Plain lacings at the knee bespoke a more serious nature than most present and adorned a calf that surpassed even Lord John's. Turning to join the gentleman in the dance, she found him studying her. As they danced, a strange spell grew between them. Hands were held longer than necessary at the turns; their eyes connected at each revolution of the set.

"My lady." Lord John appeared at Barry's side at the dance's close. "We feared you lost."

She gave herself a mental shake and turned to him. "In truth I was, and in some danger, but this gentleman kindly rescued me."

"It was my pleasure." Taking her hand, he raised it to his lips before moving away.

"Do you know the gentleman?" Barry asked Lord John as she watched her champion depart with uncertain reluctance.

"I fear not, my lady," he answered and took her to Glenna.

At a distance the man who had accosted Barry twitched his lace-edge sleeves nervously before a tall, slim gentleman whose hawkish features were scarce concealed by his mask. "But it could not be helped. I thought you close, as agreed, sir," he stammered.

"Never seen any take much note of a lone lady before. Perhaps he knows her?"

"For your sake it had best be but chance." Alfred Looten reined in his desire to sharply cuff the bumbler. His plan to gain Lady Gromley's favor by rescuing her had been spoiled. "Be gone," he ordered, his eyes following Barry.

The evening passed in a whirl of dances, Barry's partners ever changing. For the most part she could only guess who the masked gentlemen were, and although certain her popularity was once again Glenna's doing, she found herself enjoying the attention, her earlier apprehensions forgotten.

As a lively gigue drew to a close, Barry's partner graciously offered to fetch her an ice. He was gone only moments when she was claimed and led to the assembling set for a gavotte. All about men and women were engaged in excited conspiratorial whispers, but she paid little heed. Fanning herself, Barry studied her partner and decided it was the young Lord Sefton.

The dance began and as it appeared an ordinary gavotte, the continued air of expectancy puzzled Barry, as did the great attention some were paying to partners other than their own. In mid-dance the music halted momentarily and there was an instant melee—the ladies as well as the gentlemen seeking different partners. Bewildered, Barry stumbled and would have fallen but for a strong, slim hand on her elbow staying her.

"Thank you," she said meekly, her cheeks bright red with embarrassment beneath the domino.

"Shall we dance?"

The stranger's deep, quiet voice stirred her heart.

Barry recognized the same warmth she had experienced earlier. She did not need the blue domino to tell her that her rescuer was coming to her aid once again. "Yes." She drew in a deep breath, attempting to quiet her heart, and cursed the mask the hid his features. At the end of the gavotte, she pushed down the strange reluctance to part from him. "Sir, I thank you once again." Barry curtsied.

"I am not accustomed to the ways of London, I fear, nor to this amount of dancing." Barry fluttered her fan before her face, astounded to find herself flirting.

His lips curved into a wry smile. "You need some refreshment." A wave of his hand brought a footman to their side and he handed her a glass, his fingers brushing hers.

Drinking deeply, Barry tried to shake off the light-headedness swirling through her. Her heart began beating more quickly as he continued to gaze at her.

"The air has become overheated with this crush," the gentleman observed nonchalantly. "The gardens await with refreshing breath."

"It is warm." Barry plied her fan faster, far too aware of him. Her pulse leaped as he took her hand and placed it on his arm, then covered it with his own. "I—I do not—" She scanned the throng for sign of Glenna.

He skillfully guided her toward the gardens. With a last glance over her shoulder, Barry acquiesced.

Glenna noted her friend's newest escort. She tapped Lord John's arm with her fan. "The gentleman in the blue domino with Lady Gromley—there." She pointed them out as they neared the door. "Do you know who he is?"

"Why, no. How can I? He is masked," Lord John said with a laugh. "But I believe he is the chap who rescued her earlier this evening."

"We both know over half of this throng, masked or not," Glenna returned curtly. "Please learn who he is."

Struck by the unusual sharpness of her tone, Lord John nodded and moved away at once to do as bid.

Tapping her foot impatiently, Glenna watched the two disappear through the doors and began to question the wisdom of bringing Barry, so innocent of the ways of a masque, to Raneleagh.

Outside the Rotunda in the cold, crisp air, Barry shivered and drew her domino more closely about her.

"You will take a chill," the gentleman said and moved closer.

"Truly, sir," Barry said, disturbed as much by the strangely familiar ring of the man's voice as by the knowledge that she should never have left the masque with him.

"My lord," he corrected. "You have the mischance of being escorted by a peer of the realm," he said cynically.

The sarcasm drew her eyes to his.

"There are those who would say it was no rescue at all." The flickering lantern light heightened the leanness of his features, which showed below the mask. His eyes suddenly filled with pain. "You remind me of someone," he said wearily. The arm about her shoulders drew her closer. "Your voice—your eyes."

Mesmerized by his gaze, wondering why she was not frightened, Barry did not read his intent until he bent his head to hers. She stiffened but allowed him to kiss her and instantly regretted it when she found herself tempted to respond to his gentleness. Memory of another time, another place surged through her and shame rushed to the fore. "You are—mistaken in me, my lord," she cried, trying to step back.

His grip tightened.

"I—I must return to my friends." Her voice wavered beneath his stare. "This is—is highly improper."

His bitter laugh startled her. "You even speak the words I imagine she would say."

"My lord." Barry's voice quavered. "I am sorry if some—some lady has played false with you, but I had no such intent. I am newly come to London and was not aware—" Her voice trailed off as his hands left her shoulders and moved to her mask.

After a moment's hesitation, the gentleman raised her hood and laid it back. When the lantern light played across Barry's features, he released it as if it were a firebrand.

"My lord," Barry said softly, stricken by the unbearable pain she read in his eyes, his stance. She reached out to him.

"My God! It is you," he said. "Barry." His lips compressed into a thin line and then he swung away wildly, blindly brushing past a lady and gentleman in his path.

Glenna rushed to Barry's side. "There you are. Come inside before you are as frozen as when we first met," she said lightly, attempting to jest. Her twitter was cut short by the white-faced look of her friend. "Let me help you with your mask." Glenna reached up to replace the domino.

"Who is he? The man who hurried past you. Do you know him?" Barry managed through a constricted throat. Numb, she allowed the domino to be tied in place.

"What, that bloke?" Lord John echoed, joining the women. "Odd his not returning my greeting," he snorted. "Seemed friendly enough when I met him."

"Who is he?" Barry repeated.

"The most eligible man in all of London, as you

ladies would say." Lord John smiled. "The Earl of Prideau, newly come from the King's victorious army against the French and savages in America."

His smile quickly faded as Barry wavered before him. He leaped forward to catch her. "Really, now, why do all you women have to swoon over a bloody earl?" Lord John said, carrying Barry to a nearby bench.

"Hush," Glenna said. "Do not gape at her. She has had a terrible shock. Why, she almost wed the man twelve years ago," she explained, fumbling in her muff for her hartshorne.

Lord John shrugged. "And?"

Glenna shook her head. "Men." Finding the hartshorne at last, she held it beneath Barry's nose.

Chapter Three

Glenna turned angrily to the maid. "Go to your duties."

The young maid, newly come from the country, withered beneath her mistress' anger.

Barry took the petticoat from the young girl. "I shall finish my packing. Go now," she added gently, and the maid scuttled out of the bedchamber.

The two women stared at each other across the littered bed.

Barry began folding the undergarment. "I have written to the children. I am going home, Glenna."

"But what of our visit with Lady Montague?" her friend said calmly, her burst of temper now firmly under control.

"You shall make the necessary apologies. I have been away from home far too long." Thinking of Prideau, she bit her lip and jammed her petticoat into the portmanteau.

Glenna walked around the bed, carefully considering her next action. That Barry had swooned after meeting Prideau and then had sworn it was only the heat had been enough to whet her curiosity. She had failed, however, to extract the smallest detail. "If you cannot be persuaded to remain in London," she began carefully, "may I visit Gromley Hall?"

"Oh, Glenna." Barry dropped the garment she held and stepped forward, drawing her friend into a warm embrace. "I have been a terrible trial to you—ungrateful, wretched." She released her. "I realize it was nonsense for me to accuse you of directing—of directing Prideau the night of the masque," she said hurriedly and sought another garment to fold.

Glenna grasped at the opportunity. "Why were you so dismayed at meeting him? It is not unusual for a couple pledged as young as you were to part. Did he behave improperly?"

"Nothing happened." Barry continued her packing with renewed vehemence, her movements quick, her features grim.

"But you swooned."

Barry dissolved into tears. Sitting on the bed, she daubed at her eyes. "What a sorry creature I have become. What you must think of me, bursting into tears for the least thing."

Putting an arm around Barry's shoulders, Glenna gave her a comforting squeeze. "It is only justice. It was often the other way about when we were at school."

"That was girlish giddiness." Barry laughed weakly. "And also theatrics." Her smile gained substance. "Like the time you released a mouse during your conference with the headmistress and dance master."

"Fainting in that gentleman's arms taught me a valuable lesson," Glenna said seriously to her.

"Aye, to pick a stronger gentleman."

"Being plopped onto the floor is not genteel." The

other grimaced. "And Lord John almost gave you like treatment."

Barry lowered her gaze.

Glenna took her hand. "It is not like you to be so easily overwrought." She saw the strain of the last twelve years in Barry's eyes. "You rescued me when we were silly girls. For all my foolishness, I never betrayed that; it is the same now."

Barry took a deep breath. "It is but sentimental foolishness. . . ." She sighed. "I have often wondered what poor sort of female I am to be so haunted by a lost love." She smiled wanly at Glenna's puzzlement. "You alone knew of the pledge between—between Prideau and myself—of the promise rose. I meant to tell Father, but he was so busy." Barry fell silent. She wiped away a fresh tear.

"I wrote faithfully for a year and into the second." Her voice faded. "Never once did Prideau answer. I finally sent a missive begging him to write no matter what." She sniffed loudly. "It was madness on my part, but when he did not answer I imagined him killed by those barbarous red-skinned people in that land. Then shortly before Father's death I read the notice of his betrothal in the *London Times.*"

"Oh, Barry—"

"You need not tell me what a fool I was—have been," she said bitterly. "He must have enjoyed laughing at my pathetic notes." She rose with a shaky laugh. "It is all so ridiculous. I am nine and twenty and carrying on like my stepdaughter of six and ten." She looked at Glenna. "I admit I have been easily upset of late. The barrister was shockingly abrupt about Gromley's debts. Meeting Prideau as I did was an added jolt."

Realizing her friend's composure was fragile, Glenna

agreed glibly, "Of course. I will send a maid to assist you. My carriage will take you to the coaching yard."

"Thank you for—for all you have done."

"It is you who have earned my gratitude." Glenna airily waved her hand. Kissing Barry's cheek, she said, "Have a safe journey," and fluttered away.

Informed that the coach would not be leaving for a half hour, Barry decided to take a walk. Her thoughts were troubled with Prideau and she wanted to erase him from them.

A few blocks beyond the intersection to the east of the coaching yard, she continued walking aimlessly, paying little heed to her surroundings. Barry walked past a large brick building, never seeing the man approaching from the other side.

Nor did Prideau see her until he was a stride away and then his momentum made it impossible to stop. Reaching out with both arms to keep the woman from falling, he caught her against him and held on tightly to keep them both from falling.

For a long moment after they stopped stumbling, both stood perfectly still. Feeling the man's hands eased from her shoulders, Barry began to release the instinctive hold she had taken about his waist. She looked up at the same moment Prideau looked down.

Both froze. Seeing Barry's eyes wide with shock, he could not be angry, but only think of how vulnerable she looked. A groan stirred deep within him as the desire to kiss her grew almost unbearable.

Barry's heart had leapt into her throat upon recognizing him. A part of her told her to pull her hands away, to step back. But her heart longed for this closeness. She realized with a mental start that the spicy cologne he was wearing was the same as that long ago magical evening.

"Barry," he said softly.

"Prideau," she whispered.

"Kiss the woman and be done with it!" a passer-by called out raucously, causing the couple to spring apart.

They stared at one another, blinking their way back to the present.

"I am sorry—" they both began and both halted.

Barry twisted the cord of her reticule nervously. "I was not watching where I was going."

"I was distracted," Prideau said tightly. *Distracted with thoughts of you.* "Are you hurt?"

"No," she said. A coach horn sounded in the distance. "I must go," Barry said backing away from him. "I am going home to Gromley Hall." She turned and ran toward the call of the horn.

Prideau stood watching her. He told himself to be angry that she could still affect him so but regret for what could have been overpowered that emotion.

"I still do not understand why Barry bolted back to the Cotswolds so suddenly," Lord John asked obdurately that evening at the Devonshire soiree.

Glenna gazed at him over her silk fan for a long second. "Lord John, I do believe I require some refreshment. It is ghastly warm." She fluttered her lashes. "Please?"

"Warm? But we just arrived." His response shifted beneath the threat of her pursed lips. "Of course."

Watching him go, Glenna irritatedly fanned herself. *First you let Barry try your temper and now poor Lord John.* "Careless of you," she said. Lightly tapping her fan in the palm of her gloved hand, she began to stroll.

"Why, Lord Sefton, what a pleasure to see you." Glenna deftly took the startled young man's arm.

"Good evening." The young peer swallowed hard.

After chatting for a time she said lightly, "I understand you are related to Prideau."

"He is a dark one. It is still difficult to think of him as the earl, although it is more than a year since his elder brother was taken by a virulent fever."

Glenna duplicated his frown. "How unfortunate."

"But Prideau lived through the taking of Quebec," Sefton continued, his chest puffing larger with each nod of the attractive woman on his arm. "He was wounded. Still recovering, I gather."

Glenna glanced coyly at his lordship. "How comes it that he is still unwed? I had heard he was betrothed years ago."

"That was forced by his father and came to naught. He was but a younger son then, and she chose another with funds when he kept delaying their marriage."

Much later in the evening, after bidding Lord John a good night, Glenna sat brushing her hair. She went over all she knew about Prideau. She had spoken with Lady Agatha, Prideau's cousin who had hinted at information. "On the morrow I shall call upon Lady Agatha and learn the truth of the matter. Then I shall visit Barry."

The jolting of the unsprung coach jarred Barry awake. Looking out the window, she saw the sharp hills of Chalford Road and knew they would soon be in flatter grazing land. She would be at the drop-off point for Gromley Hall in a few hours. A heavy sigh escaped. Thoughts of Prideau haunted her.

Alighting from the mud-spattered coach, she

smiled at the old man beside the small wagon known as a tilbury.

"Good day, my lady." He pulled at his forelock, an ancient custom she had unsuccessfully tried to break in the past.

Barry allowed him to hand her up. "I hope you have not had to wait for too many days."

"Only three, my lady. Passing fair," he said on the reliability of the coaching schedules.

They traveled wordlessly, the clop of the hooves beating a welcoming rhythm that faded when Gromley Hall appeared before them. The Cotswold limestone of the center square was a warm gold in the afternoon sun. The two companion wings, added in the mid-fifteenth century, did not have the warmth of the original stone and looked but poor relations clustered about a wealthy protector. Barry smiled as the tilbury came up the curving drive.

"Welcome home, my lady." Tafte, the family butler, greeted his mistress.

"Has Lord Gromley returned from school?" she asked, handing him her travel cloak and gloves.

"Only yesterday," he answered. "We had looked for your return before that."

"The roads were very bad. Is Miss Pamela home?"

"Yes, she returned five days ago, but is out riding. Lord Patrick is somewhere on the grounds."

"See to my baggage and ask Cook to serve an early supper."

"Yes, my lady."

As she walked from the dark entry hall, Barry's steps were halted by shouts just outside the doors. Recognizing her stepson's voice, she smiled.

"Barry!" Patrick burst into the entry hall. He ran forward, then halted awkwardly, conscious that he was mud-spattered. "It is good to have you home—to be home," he said.

"Yes, very good." Barry extended her hand and was rewarded with a stiff pumping and a warm smile. "I'm sorry I was not here to welcome you. I stayed in London longer than—"

"No need to fret on my account. I told Pamela you deserved a holiday after—well, you know."

Her heart went out to this awkward lad, forced to manhood by his father's death. He had proven a ray of sunshine for her, and she had been deeply saddened when he left for school that past fall.

"Come, you have much to tell me. What subjects have you mastered? Were you treated well?" Patrick's boyish laugh tempted Barry to tousle his dark blond hair.

Then Patrick fell silent and straightened, suddenly seeming very mature. "And you have much to tell me. What did Father's barrister have to say?" A grin broke his serious expression. "I'm so glad Father wed you before he rushed that last fence." He gave her a quick kiss on the cheek.

We shall speak after supper," she told him. *If only Patrick was not so trusting*, she thought while watching him mount the stairs. *And Pamela was—well, Pamela.*

"I don't care what you say, Pamela. Barry's not done anything wrong," Patrick said angrily inside the salon.

"You are a simple child, Patrick. Why do you not listen to me?" Pamela stamped her foot angrily. *If only Alfred would tell Patrick how Barry trapped our father into marriage*, she thought, *but he is right that my brother would only tell Barry. And that our meetings should be kept secret.* A shiver of excitement ran through her at how daring it was.

"You are only six and ten," Patrick said. "Ever since Mother died you have tried to order everyone about. You are jealous. Admit it. Barry has done well for you. Even Mother could not convince Father to let you attend that fancy school at Cheltenham."

"She only wed Father to have his money and was glad to be rid of me. You shall see her true colors when Gromley Hall is no longer ours," Pamela said, remembering how her own heart had been broken when Lord Looten swore Barry meant to make Gromley Hall her own no matter what the cost.

Out in the corridor, Barry bit her lip. *How close to the truth and yet how far from it this young woman is*, she thought. *How am I to make her understand?*

After coughing loudly, Barry entered the salon. She paused inside the door, met by two vastly different attitudes—one trusting, the other hostile—and she knew she could not reveal the extent of Lord Gromley's gambling debts.

"The conditions of your lands and finances cannot displease you." The elderly solicitor studied the younger man, who was usually more attentive.

"What did you say?" Prideau asked absentmindedly, slowly flexing his left leg.

At five and thirty, the fourth Earl of Prideau was a somber, handsome man. The close cut of his brown corduroy short-skirted coat, denuded of the customary fobs and lacings, set off his admirable form. Matching muscle-hugging breeches and well-polished riding boots had drawn many a female eye to the self-assured visage beneath the beaver tricorne during his early morning ride.

"The wound still pains you?"

Prideau dismissed his concern. "Seldom." His mind jumped to the reports just given. "All is satisfactory."

"You might tell your agent that," the solicitor offered. "You had such a dark look I imagine he fears dismissal."

"My mind was on another matter." Prideau grimaced, then a smile eased the cynical cast. "I shall take your advice."

The solicitor remained silent, his fingertips poised together. "Will you take it on another point, my lord?" he asked.

"Surely I do not strike fear in you?" Prideau asked. "You have no marriageable daughter, so you need not fear offending me."

For a moment the solicitor debated commenting on this worrisome change in Prideau's manner but said instead, "I would wish you had wed before coming to the title."

"It was not for my lack of effort," Prideau said bitterly. The words brought Barry vividly to his mind.

"I fear it would displease you." The solicitor gave him a wry smile. "But the house of Prideau must have an heir, and many women would willingly accept that duty."

"Willingly," said Prideau, more open with this trusted family advisor than he had been with anyone since attaining the earldom. "The lecture is not needed." He thought again of the painful chance meetings with Barry. "I need to refresh my spirit. What would you recommend?"

"Bath is the favorite watering place this time of year," the solicitor said. "It may help your leg as well."

Prideau gave him a mock salute. "It is also the largest marriage mart in all of England." He left considering the suggestion carefully. Among so many women perhaps he could forget the one haunting him.

Chapter Four

Satisfied with her missive to Glenna, Barry sanded it and then applied wax and seal. "Send this to be posted at once," she instructed her butler, Tafte. "I shall be going out with Lord Patrick and will not return until late in the afternoon."

"Yes, my lady. Shall I have Cook delay luncheon for you?"

"No, we shall take some fruit and cheese with us. But do tell her to serve supper an hour early. Has Miss Pamela breakfasted?"

"Miss is in the breakfast room now, my lady."

She dismissed him and went to her bedchamber to change into her riding habit. While she dressed, she mentally balanced the accounts of the estate which she had been studying with the estate manager since her return. She reminded herself that she meant to speak with him about the new groom in the stables she had noticed since returning from London.

If only things had gone as well with Pamela. The girl had been outraged upon being informed that she would not have a season. She had blamed Barry, had

44

hinted she knew all. When asked to explain, she had become sullenly silent. That war still raged.

And Lord James, co-guardian to her stepchildren as well as a widowed neighbor with a brood of his own children, had called. Luckily Patrick had distracted him.

If Glenna proves agreeable, she thought, drawing on her gloves, *two of the problems would be solved.* Barry was unable to decide whether Pamela's continued hostility or Lord James' heavy-handed courting was more distressing.

But even the scene with Pamela, and Lord James' refusal to be hinted away had not turned her mind from Prideau. He haunted her dreams, both day and night.

Barry shook herself and thought instead of Lord James' insistence she tell her stepchildren of the gambling debts. Patrick had taken the economies of retrenchment well.

At the conclusion of Barry's account of the estate's debt, Patrick had risen and squared his shoulders manfully. "It is unfortunate but not the worst news." He looked from Barry to his sister. "We still have Gromley Hall and it looks to be an excellent year for the crops and cattle."

Barry smiled gratefully and turned with anxious expectancy to Pamela. "Surely you can see why it would be best to delay your coming out until we will be better able to—"

"Next year!" Pamela was livid. "Patrick," she swung around to face her brother, "now can you see what she is doing?"

Taken aback by his sister's vehemence, he protested, "Barry is managing matters as best she can."

"I should say she is. Filling her coffers at our expense. She is in league with the barrister."

"Pamela, I don't think—"

"Listen to me. Father always insisted on the best. He served his guests only the finest foods and wines. Then, when he is dead only a few months, *she* begins to dismiss footmen, maids, and grooms. I tell you, she means to take everything."

"You are overwrought, Pamela," Barry said softly. "I can send to London for the documents to prove that I have spoken the truth. Or you may speak with Lord James. He is co-guardian and knows of these matters. His consent must be had for each new action taken on estate affairs."

"And he is firmly in your pocket," Pamela sneered. "I have no doubt you have arranged the matter well."

Thinking back on that conversation, Barry realized she thought the girl was being schooled in her suspicions; that her behavior was being guided. But by whom and why?

This new dimension to Pamela's hostility was the deciding factor in Barry's decision to write Glenna. If she agreed to Barry's proposal, a brief stay in Bath with a satisfactory coming out for Pamela could be had.

With this comforting thought, Barry strode from her chamber. After a brief stop in the breakfast room to tell Pamela she would return in time to help with her new gown, she went out and found mounts awaiting but Patrick nowhere in sight.

The new groom she had noted earlier was adjusting the girth on Patrick's favorite gelding. He hurriedly finished. "Morning, my lady." He bobbed a hasty bow.

Barry smiled to ease his evident discomfit. "Good

morning. Where has Lord Patrick gone?" she asked, checking her saddle.

"He went to fetch something, my lady." Edging away, the groom pointed to Patrick's approach with obvious relief.

"Good morning, Barry. It is a fine morning," Patrick said.

"Yes, indeed," she replied.

Patrick swung into the saddle while the groom helped Barry onto her sidesaddle. "Where are we to go first?"

She arranged her skirts while settling comfortably in the saddle. "I thought we would check the cottagers to the west, then the summer pastures, and perhaps take in the grain fields on our way back to the Hall."

"Lord James hinted that you take far more interest in the land than Father ever did," Patrick told her as they rode from the Hall. "Now I know what he meant."

"The land can only return what one puts in it. It is best you learn the duties that you will face," Barry told him. "Then you will see that it is not you alone the land supports."

"Surely some unfortunate popinjay will take Pamela off my hands?" He rolled his eyes.

Barry smiled wryly. "Let us hope it is other than a popinjay." After a brief pause she continued, "Enough of such matters. I'll race you to the old oak at the turn."

"It is done." They were off.

After watching them leave from her bed chamber window, Pamela hurried to the stables. Once mounted she took the short path to the property line between

Gromley and Looten Loft as she had each day after meeting Alfred Looten by accident the first day home.

"Pamela," Looten greeted her, sounding relieved. "I feared you would not come again today." He dismounted.

"I could not come sooner with my stepmother home."

"It is just as I told you," Looten said lifting her down from her saddle. His hands lingered on her waist. "You are so beautiful."

Pamela blushed and stepped back. He unsettled her, thrilled her. The secrecy of their meetings lent a romantic air to their time together. "Patrick will not listen to me," she told him. "You must speak with Lord James."

Looten took her hand. "He disliked my father—he will not listen to me. And he wishes to marry your stepmother. He may be in on the plan with her—nothing is beyond her."

"I know," said Pamela.

"You must be strong, my dear. She will betray herself. Something will happen to Patrick—an 'accident' of the dangerous sort."

"You must—" Pamela began.

Looten's grip tightened. "No," he said, then softened his grip and expression. "We dare not let anyone know I am trying to help you, Pamela. They would forbid us to ever see one another.

"Give me your pledge that you will not reveal that we have met even if we see one another in public. I dare not tell you what your stepmother may do if she learns her plans are known." Looten put a finger beneath her chin and raised her face. "Do you understand?"

Pamela blinked back a tear and nodded.

*　*　*

Shielding her eyes against the mid-afternoon sun, Barry surveyed the fields of grain.

"Looks like a bloody good stand," Patrick said, imitating the Baron.

"Yes, thank the Lord," Barry agreed. "The fleece this year should be excellent too."

Patrick turned to her. "You shouldn't let Pamela worry you. Beneath all her whoops she is a good sort. She carried on well while Mother was ill.

"Last fall I thought she had admitted to herself that she liked you and was but waiting for a chance to say so without losing face," he said. "But she's changed since she came home." Patrick shook his head worriedly.

"I've hopes of righting things," Barry assured him. "Pamela is going through the difficult years. You will soon face similar problems."

"If you mean sighing and giggling about girls, you need have no fear," the young lad said. "I've taken my lessons well from the older lads at school and have no wish to make a bloody fool of myself over a girl."

Restraining her smile, Barry urged her mount forward. "Time to return to Gromley."

"Not so soon," Patrick protested, then broke into a grin. "Why don't we gallop to see if those violets you love are in bloom?" Before she could object he called out the hunt challenge, "So ho!" and galloped away.

Bringing her riding crop down, Barry gave chase. She reveled in the ride as her mare gained on Patrick's. Suddenly she froze.

Patrick, still many paces ahead, began to fall, his saddle slipping to one side. She watched him waver wildly, then in agonizing slow motion fall beneath his startled mount's hooves. The lad was left unnaturally sprawled on the grassy plain.

An agonized scream stuck in Barry's throat. She drew her mount to a rearing halt and leaped haphazardly from the sidesaddle. "Patrick! Patrick!" She knelt, turning his grass and mud-stained face gently upward. His steady heartbeat freed her own. Checking his legs, Barry found no damage, but the unnatural bend of his left arm bespoke broken bones.

The lad stirred. A low groan escaping, he shifted slightly. His eyelids fluttered then opened. "Barry?" he said, trying to focus his gaze. "What happened?"

"Lie still," she told him. "I do not know how badly you are hurt."

Patrick winced. "My arm?"

"It is broken," she answered. "Why don't you try to move your legs? Good." She sighed in relief. "If only we had some way of getting back to Gromley." Barry eyed her lone mount. "Yours ran off. One hopes running home," she said, tearing at the lower flounce of her petticoat. "Then someone will come looking for us."

"What happened? It was all so sudden."

"Your saddle's girth must have snapped. The new groom will be dismissed for not having seen it was too worn."

Patrick attempted a wan smile. "Next time I shall check it myself, just as you do."

She rose and retrieved their riding crops. "These will have to do to brace your arm. You may scream if you like," Barry told him.

Patrick gamely clenched his teeth while she bound his arm with the two riding crops and strips of her petticoat. Then she fashioned a sling.

After it was in place, Barry helped him to his feet, supporting him once he was standing. "We can't de-

pend upon your gelding reaching Gromley. We had
best begin walking."

"But we have yours—" he began.

"I am not strong enough to lift you up."

"Then let's get to it," he said.

"We must go back to where we left the grain fields.
They won't know we have come this way." She
frowned, but quickly smiled when he looked at her.
"Help will come before we have gone a dozen fur-
longs," she added, hoping her words held truth.

It was well over two hours before a rescue party
found them. The broken arm had swollen and only grit
was keeping Patrick on his feet despite frequent rests.

Dispatching one of the men to fetch the physician, Barry saw her stepson comfortably settled in a
straw-filled wagon and the slow trek back to Gromley
continued.

Looking up as the Hall came into view, Barry found
her relief tempered by the sight of Pamela poised dramatically in the Hall's open doors. When the field
wagon stopped at the foot of the steps, the young
woman descended with a flurry of hoops, petticoats,
and shrieks.

"For God's sake, Pamela, I'm all right," Patrick said
through tightly-clenched teeth. His eyes went beseech-
ingly to his stepmother.

Barry accepted the butler's hand down and calmly
ordered him to have Patrick taken to his bedchamber.
This done, she turned to Pamela. "It is only a broken
arm. Calm yourself."

The young woman gulped down her wailing, looking wild-eyed at her stepmother. "It's true! All of it is
true. You mean to kill him."

"Pamela." Barry stepped closer but the girl jumped back.

"Do you not see," she shouted to the men standing about the wagon. "She means to have Gromley all to herself."

Patrick attempted to reach for his sister, but fainted.

"Calm yourself for your brother's sake," Barry said angrily, and took a hold of her arm. "Take him inside at once," she ordered and pulled Pamela with her as she followed them.

Those remaining about the wagon stared at one another in wordless wonder. A bell-like voice startled them.

"Could one of you please assist me in alighting?" Glenna McDowell asked in her tinkling voice, leaning her dainty straw-bonneted head out of the window of her traveling coach.

Chapter Five

Three days later Barry drew a deep breath as she tried once again to reason with Pamela. "I have no intention of forcing you to do anything. If only you would realize that your outbursts are harmful to both of us. It will be best if you go to your aunt's—at least for a time."

"I will not abandon Patrick," Pamela said. Then she stilled and slowly assumed a false calm. "I will be silent as you wish. But I *know* what you are doing. Be certain that I shall tell everyone if anything should happen to my brother."

Pamela walked haughtily to the door, then looked back. "There was another like you. The second Viscountess Gromley, also a second wife." She sneered. "That one killed her husband in 1654. When she tried to do the same to his son, she was caught and hung—just as you shall be."

Barry felt a chill to the depth of her bones. *She honestly believes what she's saying.* Placing a hand fearfully over her heart as Pamela flounced out of the salon, she whispered, "Has she gone mad?"

Glenna sailed into the salon. "My dear, that girl is

becoming a shrew. And that is sad because she would be quite a belle *if* she would but add some sweetness to her temperament."

"Pamela really is not like this," Barry said weakly. "I have handled the situation badly from the first. I never dreamed her resentment could take such a turn."

"You had best fear for your neck," Glenna said quietly. "My coachman said Lord Patrick's saddle's cinch was cut."

Barry blanched. "Dear God, who would do such a thing?"

"After the girl's ravings—do you think her feelings strong enough for her to risk her brother's life?"

"Pamela is headstrong and willful but not—no, never." Barry shook her head. "I shall have Lord James, who is guardian of the children with me, investigate."

"Lord James? Your persistent suitor?"

Barry grimaced. "Earnest, unfortunately, is a truer description. He and Pamela are why I wrote you."

"So our stay in Bath is to be an escape that settles both problems? This is much more like the old Barry." Glenna arched an assessing brow.

Barry blushed. "It is far better than Lord James' solution. He wished her coming-out to be at his home."

"And before that ball was over, he would be announcing that you are to wed him. Heaven forbid such an admirable design." Glenna sank back in her chair. "Oh, swallow the frown. Surely you have made your feelings clear to the fellow?" She ran a finger contemplatively around the edge of her goblet. "Would it not solve many of your problems to marry him?"

"Never," Barry answered adamantly. "Nor will I see Pamela sold in marriage to some fool just because he offers for her. That is why we shall go to Bath." *And far from Prideau.*

"The stay in Bath is acceptable to Lord James?"

"Of course. And with the small loan you have agreed to give me, we need wait only for Patrick's arm to improve before leaving."

"You have thought this out very carefully." Glenna studied her, then broke into a mischievous grin. "Has the thought entered your mind that we might find *you* a husband in Bath?"

Barry shook her head. "I shall never wed again."

The morning was crisp, the sky brilliantly blue as Barry galloped through an open meadow on the Gromley Estate. She rode hard, trying to drive thoughts of Prideau from her mind. For several glorious moments she reveled in the fine day, the rush of air, the freedom of being away from everyone.

As her mare started up a rise, Barry slowly drew her in, stopping at the top between two thick plantings of trees. She bit her lip. *Someone has to be prompting Pamela in her attacks. It is not like her.*

Barry turned around at the sound of an approaching horse. She caught her breath as a horseman emerged at the bottom of the rise, his figure immediately recognizable.

Prideau?! What brings him here? Why is he on Gromley land? A horrid misgiving slithered into her mind. *Is he—could he be responsible for Pamela's changed demeanor?* She sat rigidly in the saddle as he neared.

"Good morning, my lady," Prideau greeted her, flicking a hand toward the brim of his beaver hat. "You still ride very well."

Barry tried to push her suspicion aside. "Good

morning, my lord," she returned, her tone cold and formal. "What brings you here?" she asked. Accusation tinted her words.

Prideau studied her. *You bring me here,* he admitted silently. His gaze caressed her dark brown hair, lingered on her face, a face he had memorized twelve years ago and still found fascinating. Then he saw the shadows beneath her eyes and anger surged at what had caused them. *I should not, must not care*, he thought and could not prevent a bitter bark of laughter from escaping.

Barry tried to look away but she was held by her own fascination. Her heart had begun thudding as soon as she saw him. She tried to think of something to say but was too overwhelmed by his brooding closeness.

Seeing something like fear wash across Barry's features, Prideau winced. *You were a fool to come*, he told himself. *She is the one who broke our betrothal, not you.* But he could not rein away.

"I must get back to Gromley Hall," Barry said nervously. "They will be expecting me." She began to rein her horse about only to find Prideau's blocking her way. His hand clasped the one in which she held her reins. Barry trembled at his touch, a longing sweeping through her.

Prideau experienced the same but was not surprised by the intensity of his response. It had been the same even at the masque before he knew who she was. The devils that drove him to deny any feeling for her receded beneath a stronger force. Prideau leaned forward and brushed her lips with a kiss that feathered a question. "Why did you do it, Barry?" he asked in a husky whisper.

Barry knew she should pull away; that his hold was

light and she would be able to. But her yearning was too strong. She returned the kiss.

Pulling back abruptly, Prideau's features turned stormy as he released her hands. "This was a mistake," he said. "I will not trouble you again." With that, he galloped away.

Barry watched Prideau until he was out of sight. His behavior was beyond her comprehension. He was attracted to her but something else was at work. *Why this mysterious appearance? What did he mean?* she asked over and over as she rode back to Gromley Hall.

Prideau rode hard for several minutes before he thought to spare his mount. Reining to a slower pace, he calmed himself. He had meant only to see what she had gained by not marrying him, to look at Gromley Hall and then go on to a friend's house where his coach awaited to take him to Bath.

But seeing Barry ride out as he approached Gromley Hall, the same force that had brought him to pass by Gromley compelled him to follow her. He had meant to demand an explanation for their broken betrothal but had lost all power of reasoning when he touched her and breathed in the faint lily of the valley scent he would always think of as hers. She *broke the betrothal*, he reminded himself. A moment later he wondered what emotion he had seen in her eyes. Eyes that had once looked at him with love. Could it have been fear? *Why do I torment both of us? I must not see her again*, he sternly told himself, but in his heart he hoped fate had other plans.

Barry was very glad to have the distraction of preparations for their journey to Bath. The meeting on the rise came often to her dreams. Its ending varied between reality and wishful thinking. At times she awoke with a fearful start and others with the surety that Prideau loved her. Working to exhaustion had become her only means to escape thinking of him.

Barry glanced out the coach window—they had left Gromley Hall two days ago—and saw the luxuriant green shawl and bejeweled spring flowers of the hills along the Fosse Way near Bath.

Glancing at Pamela, she was pleased to see her stepdaughter happily perusing a tour guide. Against it when first told they were going to Bath, Pamela had grown enthusiastic when called upon to choose gowns and all the accompanying articles.

Patrick tugged at Barry's sleeve. "Look. Rabbits!" He pointed out her window with his good hand. "There."

She shook her head. "Hare hunts are past for this year."

"Not if Lord James sees they are eating his crops," the lad answered. Grimacing, he raised the tightly wrapped splint on his left arm. "By the time we return I will not have this."

"Even if Lord James has a summer hunt, you will not take part," she told him.

"You haven't let me do anything since the accident. If all I am to be allowed to do is sit in my chamber I had best go back to Gromley," he said.

Glenna patted his shoulder. "There shall be plenty for you to do, Lord Patrick."

"In a week or two perhaps," Barry said. "When the physician says it is safe to remove the splint."

Pamela raised her eyes from the Bath and Bristol guide. "We shall be far too busy shopping, drinking water in the Pump Room, and taking part in the Parades to entertain you, Patrick."

Restraining her frown at his sister's rudeness, Barry told him, "You shall attend the theater with us."

"And the dances if you wish," Glenna added. "The second benches are for the chil—for young people."

"Dances? Ugh!" Patrick shuddered. Then he straightened. "What is that? Listen to the bells. Someone must have died."

Glenna laughed. "They are ringing for us. They greet each visitor no matter what the hour. Before the last bandbox is carried into our lodgings in Queen Square, our arrival will be common knowledge." She glanced at the creamy Bath stone of the homes and businesses that they were passing. "After we are comfortably settled in our rooms, we shall see to our subscriptions."

"And they are many," Pamela said excitedly. "For the Pump Room and the assemblies and music. For the Spring Gardens—"

"Would you mind if I did not go?" Barry asked Glenna. "I am certain Pamela will be happy to go in my place."

"Oh, could I?" the young lady asked.

"Very well," Glenna said. "We shall see how full the town is of gentlemen," she said with a wink.

"I mean only to explore Mr. Wood's Circus. I have heard it is such a marvelous sweep of stone. And you may walk with me, Patrick," Barry said.

He shrugged. "At least it will get me out of my chamber."

"I do hope my butler and housekeeper have the house ready," Glenna said with a sigh.

"Surely you will check it yourself," Barry said.

"I am more likely to attend the milliner!" Glenna laughed. "Ah, there is my butler at the door." She smiled as the coach halted before the elegant façade of the north side of Queen Square.

Glenna laid a hand on Barry's arm. "It shall be just as it was when we were girls. Handsome men, dancing—" she said, her voice floating in the air.

The steep climb up Gay Street to the Circus winded Patrick, who had been forcibly idle the past three weeks. While he paused to rest, Barry admired the unbroken sweep of Bath stone.

Regaining his breath, Patrick followed her to the center of the cobbled and paved circle. "They are grim buildings but for the garlands and masks," he said of the three orders of Roman architecture rising above each other on the three separate segments of the circus' façade.

"I believe Mr. Wood meant them to represent the legend of Bladud."

"You mean the prince who was the first ever cured here?"

"Yes, while herding the swine on acorns," Barry said. "It is said he never forgave those who had banished him from his father's court because of his leprosy."

"I wouldn't forgive them either," Patrick told her. "Father always said forgiveness was for the weak."

Barry thought of her feelings for Prideau. "Forgiving is often harder than harboring resentment or hatred," she said as they neared a coach just halting before a residence. Seeing that Patrick was not paying attention, she shouted, "Look out!" But Patrick was knocked to the ground by the opening door.

"Your arm?" Barry asked, helping him up.

Embarrassed, Patrick tried to brush aside her concern. "None the worse."

"My apologies. Is the boy harmed?" Prideau's deep voice inquired politely from the open door of the coach.

"Fortunately not!" Barry snapped.

Noticing their odd expressions and the tension between them Patrick said, "I was not watching closely." When this had no effect, he added, "You have excellent horses."

The boy unheard, Prideau asked, "You are alone?"

Patrick moved protectively in front of his stepmother. "I am Lady Gromley's escort."

Prideau's eyes swung down to the lad and back to Barry. The horses shifted nervously. "I have no further need," he said, dismissing the coach, his eyes never leaving her.

Patrick read the anger on the gentleman's features and looked at his stepmother. Her dismay and an emotion he could not fathom alarmed him. He took her arm. "We must go."

Prideau's features assumed a mask of indifference. "I will escort you to your lodgings."

Barry found her voice at last. "That is not necessary." She put her hand over Patrick's.

"Is he not a bit tender for your wiles?"

Barry was puzzled, then blanched when she realized his meaning. His eyes were blazing with the condemnation she had seen at the masque. Her own flared angrily.

"Let us pass," Patrick demanded boldly.

Prideau stepped aside and watched the pair walk away. "Blast Zeus," he swore aloud, startling a pair of strolling ladies. Entering his lodging, he slammed the door behind him. "I swore I'd not see her again," he said, pacing inside his salon. The memories of their recent encounters further darkened his features.

"This time I shall not run," Prideau said, "but stay and show her how little I care. That much I owe myself," he mumbled. "She deserves no less."

But the wound so deeply buried over the years had burst to the surface in Raneleagh's Gardens—a raw, too-long festering blow to his heart, his pride. It would not permit him any rest. After all the years he still wondered what had happened.

What were the words his secretary Hawks had quoted? Prideau searched his memory: *As Prideau is a second son whose lack of fortune is well known, I have, after careful consideration decided to end any and all connection with him.* He had refused to believe it, refused to believe Barry would write to his secretary on such a personal matter. Then the man had handed him the letter—it had been written in her hand.

The hurt boiled inside Prideau. That he still desired her angered him. A gleam of revenge glittered in his dark eyes. "She shall regret having done it," he vowed.

"We shall begin on the morrow," Glenna announced, entering the salon where Barry and Patrick played backgammon.

Pamela followed close behind, her cheeks flushed with excitement. "It was wonderful! We met a Lieutenant Horne. A vastly handsome gentleman." She sighed, sitting. "He has just returned from the war in the Americas."

"And a Mr. Looten also bid us give you his compliments," Glenna said, recalling Pamela's odd reaction to the gentleman. "He asked to call when we are comfortably settled."

Pamela nervously fingered the lace on her sleeve. "He is a handsome gentleman," she said.

"I hope he has better manners than the man we encountered in the Circus this afternoon," Patrick said, rolling his dice. "He needs a lesson in civility."

"Patrick," Barry said sharply.

"Who has caused this?" Glenna asked.

"Lord Prideau," Patrick answered. Oblivious to Barry's signal, he said, "You never did say how you knew his name."

"Prideau is here?" Glenna said in feigned surprise.

"I do not like him," Patrick said. "His visage was so black I feared he would strike Barry."

Pamela stiffened at her brother's words. "Who is this Lord Prideau?"

Barry looked back to the backgammon board. "An acquaintance from long ago. He does not signify."

Giving a hoot of triumph at the result of his roll of the dice, Patrick began moving his pieces. "I win again!"

"Supper is served, my lady," the butler announced.

"Good. I am famished," Patrick said, hurrying out.

Pamela gazed questioningly at Barry, then followed.

Noticing the fine lines of strain in Barry's features, Glenna asked, "Are you well?"

"Only a bit fatigued," Barry answered, then deftly changed the subject. "Your housekeeper asked that I tell you she hired a new maid. She wanted your approval of the hire."

"I trust her judgment. If the girl is not a good worker we shall soon know it. Now, when shall we make our first appearance in the Pump Room?"

"You and Pamela can go in the morning. I do not want Patrick becoming too active until his arm is pronounced healed."

Glenna glanced at her friend. "No. There is some shopping I must do and a few calls I must make before we begin all the activities of Bath society. It will tantalize the gentlemen to dangle Pamela before them but not have her readily accessible. She is a handsome girl for all her foolishness," she continued. "I do believe that will be best."

While Glenna babbled on, Barry pondered how long she could escape going into society, how long Prideau could be avoided.

Pain knotted her stomach. Prideau's tormented eyes haunted her, puzzled her, angered her. What right had he to treat her so when it was he himself who had not been man enough to openly end his pledge to her?

Chapter Six

"Hurry, Barry," Pamela urged, helping smooth her stepmother's shot-silk gown over her panniers. "We shall be late getting to the Pump Room if we delay longer."

"Do not fret so," Barry said. "Go see if Patrick is comfortable. I shall join you downstairs."

"Do hurry," Pamela repeated, and hurried out of the bedchamber, carefully managing her newly acquired circular hoop.

An exclamation outside the door told of a near-miss between hoops. Glenna came in with a wide grin. "Your stepdaughter hardly seems the same person."

"It is a relief to see her act as any other young lady," Barry agreed. "When the splint is removed from Patrick's arm, I shall have little to worry me. But he does have a poor appetite of late. There." She turned from her looking glass, the last pin fastening the filigree lace cap to her periwig in place. "Do you think I should worry about it?"

"No," Glenna said, dismissing her concern about

Patrick. She frowned at the sober widow's cap. "Do you really feel this is necessary?"

"Most certainly," Barry answered, "I do not want to give a false impression."

"You would do better assuming a whim. I am famous for them," Glenna said with false hauteur, adjusting the silk roses on her puffed sleeves as they went down the stairs.

Barry reluctantly smiled. "Glenna, you are impossible. How have you restrained yourself since our arrival?"

"With sincerity," she replied. "Ah, Pamela, how lovely you look this morning."

The young lady's cheeks dimpled with pleasure as she walked back into the room. "May we go now?"

"Do you have your parasol?" Barry asked. "And be careful of your hoop. It is not easily managed."

"Do not forget *your* parasol," Glenna said.

Ignoring this, Barry accepted the footman's hand into the coach. "We are here to introduce Pamela, nothing more."

Glenna fluttered her fan artlessly. "Of course, my dear."

"Do the ladies and gentlemen truly bathe together?" Pamela interrupted them, her excitement at the prospects of the day overriding all else.

"Certainly," Glenna answered. "My husband always insisted we go to the King's Bath or the Queen's Bath but never to the Cross Bath."

"But I have heard they are the best," Pamela said.

"Oh, they are!" Glenna laughed. "The ladies and gentlemen there are allowed to mingle freely."

"Glenna." Barry's lips twitched nervously.

"It is harmless. What can one accomplish robed from head to toe in a covering of yellow canvas?

Dreadful stuff. I always took a beribboned nosegay from the tray."

"Tray?" Barry asked, turning her gaze from the window.

"Wooden basins for all the necessities," Glenna explained.

"Standing in warm water watching a wooden bowl float about strikes me as singularly—well, I care not if I ever attend," Barry said.

"But the basins are attached to one's waist by ribbons," Glenna said. "And if they do become free— accidentally of course," she poised her fan before continuing, "the gentlemen are always willing to assist one in retying them."

Barry scowled at her, then gazed out of the coach window. "The Pump Room at last."

Glenna led her companions into the squarish Pump Room to take part in the ritual drinking of the waters.

Pamela's smile grew brighter with each successive young man's nod as they approached the counter where glasses of water were being dispensed. "Did you ever see so many handsome gentlemen?" she whispered, returning yet another greeting.

"I did not think so many gentlemen would attend," Barry said. "Does everyone do nothing more than walk about in this circular fashion?" she asked in a low voice, accepting the glass of cloudy water from the young woman at the pump. "When can we leave?"

"Sip the water, then you may take a seat if you wish," Glenna said, dismissing her friend's question, and motioning to the seated dowagers. "Enjoy yourself. Ah, I see an acquaintance from London," she told her. "I shall be but a moment." As she walked off, Barry and Pamela were alone but a second before Alfred Looten joined them.

Mr. Looten bowed to Barry and her charge. "Lady Gromley, it is a pleasant surprise to see you again. I hope it was not ill health that confined you to your lodging."

"My health is excellent," Barry answered, warmed by the solicitude. "You have met my stepdaughter, Miss Pamela Gromley. Did you realize Mr. Looten is our neighbor?"

"Of course, Looten's Loft," Pamela replied, then hastily lowered her gaze.

"You make a most charming pair," Looten said.

"Have you been in Bath long?" Barry asked him, her surprise at Pamela's familiarity with the Loft forgotten when her gaze wandered to Glenna and the gentleman standing before her friend. Even though his back was to her, Barry recognized the stance and her heart leapt despite herself.

Beside them stood Lady Agatha, Prideau's cousin who had provided Glenna such interesting facts in London. She now smiled slyly as she introduced her cousin. "Prideau, Mrs. McDowell. I will leave you young people to converse." She held out her hand for Prideau to assist her bulky form from the chair. "The water has a simply debilitating affect," Lady Agatha said with a sigh. "But it so helps my joints." She walked off, giving Glenna an encouraging wink.

Prideau's brow furrowed in thought. "McDowell?"

"Why, Prideau, you do not recall me." Implied hurt tinged Glenna's bell-like tones. "Then the least you could do is take note of my gown." She curtsied coyly. "Is not the rose your favorite flower?"

Prideau's lips curved into a scowl. "I detest roses. Pray excuse me," he told her curtly.

Glenna laid a gloved hand on his arm. "It was presumptuous of me to claim friendship but do not go in

anger," she urged contritely, the sharpness of his reaction to her question a confirmation of her hopes that
he still loved Barry. "Forgive me. We met only at a
house party, and that long ago."

Recognition struck Prideau. "Please excuse me," he
apologized. "How is Mr. McDowell? Is he here with
you?"

"He was carried away by a fever three years ago."
Prideau began to speak but Glenna stopped him.
"There is no need for condolences," she said, studying
him carefully. "Time heals many wounds, wouldn't
you agree?" She watched something flicker in the deep
brown eyes before a smile surfaced.

"The years have been most generous to you, Mrs.
McDowell. You are more lovely than I remember."

She fluttered her lashes. "You gentlemen are all the
same. A rich widow must be forever on her guard."

"You are alone then?"

"No. I am traveling with a friend and her stepchildren. Not my usual company but amusing for the moment," Glenna answered. "And you?"

"Sadly, alone," he replied.

"That will never do," Glenna began, then flashed a
welcoming smile over his shoulder. "My friends," she
said, preventing Barry from hurrying past and turning
Prideau to face the lady, Pamela, and Looten.

Prideau turned graciously. His heart lurched despite
his firm resolution, but he managed to hold his calm
demeanor save for the flicker of a muscle along his
jaw.

Introductions were made. Pamela, blushing prettily,
bobbed a curtsy to Prideau but Barry remained aloof.

"Prideau is recently returned from the Americas
where he took part in the victory of Quebec," Glenna

said, revealing some of what she had learned from Lady Agatha. "He was wounded."

"The loss of General Wolfe was far more tragic," Prideau assured her.

"Do you know Lieutenant Horne?" Pamela inquired artlessly. "He, too, has just returned from the war in the colonies."

Catching Barry's frown at her stepdaughter's forwardness, and knowing she would dislike it, Prideau offered his arm to the girl. "You must describe him to me. Let us walk—if Lady Gromley approves." He looked at her.

"Of course," Barry said, silently disavowing the trembling of her heart.

Looten, noticing her displeasure, offered her his arm.

Flashing a grateful smile, Barry accepted. Angered at her reaction to Prideau, she was overly gracious to her escort. Nor did she note Mrs. McDowell's suddenly subdued mood.

"Glenna?" Barry asked a second time a short while later when her friend did not respond to a question.

Glenna smiled. "Yes?"

"Mr. Looten has graciously offered to escort us to the theater this evening."

"If you would like it, Barry, we shall go," she answered.

"And Miss Gromley may go with us?" Looten smiled at Barry's nod. "I shall call for all of you at six."

"Pamela, oh, Pamela," Glenna called gaily to the young lady who was passing with Prideau. "It is time we go. We did promise Patrick we would stop at the lending library."

"Patrick is my brother," Pamela told Prideau as they

joined the others. "He broke his arm in a—a riding accident and is being pampered."

"It speaks well of you to be so solicitous of him," Prideau said, eyeing Looten who was standing close to Barry. He took Pamela's hand and kissed it lightly. "Perhaps I shall see you later this evening."

"Truly, Pamela," Barry said when the young woman prattled about Looten as they relaxed in the Green Salon after returning to their lodgings. "You should restrain your enthusiasm. Before you were speaking highly of Lieutenant Horne. These gentlemen's characters are, for the most part, unknown to you—to us. They may well be encouraging false hopes."

"You are only jealous because I have made friends and because Prideau was kind to me," Pamela said.

"What nonsense," Barry scoffed. "You shall meet many fine gentlemen during our stay. It is unwise to decide on one so early, especially when you do not know him well."

Pamela smirked. "We shall see." The young lady rose. "I am going to rest. I wish to look my best for the theater."

"I doubt she shall take your advice," Glenna told Barry. "Looten is not as carefree as Lieutenant Horne but he is an acceptable suitor. Perhaps we could ask Prideau to check on Lieutenant Horne's family."

"How unfortunate *he* is in Bath," Barry said. "Did you know he would be here?"

Glenna deliberately misunderstood, fluttering her fan innocently. "Mr. Looten? How could I? I barely know the gentleman.

"And Barry," she continued, "I hardly think it wise—the way you glower at Prideau."

"Harrumph."

"We shall encounter him often. He can make matters difficult for Pamela if he should chose to do so. Bath is not London. The places of entertainment are common to all."

"I was just thinking my time would be better spent with Patrick," Barry tried to change the subject, though she realized the truth of her friend's words. "I am concerned about his listlessness since we arrived."

"Are you are afraid to speak with him?" Glenna asked.

"Afraid? Why, I find Mr. Looten attractive," Barry replied, purposely dissembling.

"Then you certainly cannot wish to avoid him." Glenna closed her trap. "Unless you do intend to wed Lord James."

Barry rose angrily. "How often do I have to tell you I intend to wed no one? No one," she repeated, and stalked from the salon.

Glenna leaned back in the settee and tapped her fan contemplatively against her chin. "Prideau and Barry have overlong memories," she said softly to herself, "which speaks of no small attachment."

Chapter Seven

The new maid bobbed a curtsy before Barry. "The housekeeper sent me to ask you look in on Lord Patrick." She lowered her eyes hastily. "He has refused to eat again."

"Tell her I shall stop by his room before we depart for the theater," Barry said, carefully completing the arrangement of the curls on her powdered periwig. Grimacing at the result, she rose and surveyed herself in the full-length looking glass. The shimmering verdant green of her sackback gown highlighted her complexion and graceful figure. She was not displeased but sighed, thinking of Glenna's sophisticated beauty.

What does it matter? Barry thought, tweaking her own vanity.

"It doesn't at all," she said aloud. Collecting her matching silk fan, she went to her stepson.

Patrick's flaccid look took on a hint of animation when she entered. "How pretty you are! I would escort you myself," he said, "if only I were not so tired,' "

Barry smiled. "There shall be ample opportunity for that. But what is this I hear about your not eating this evening?"

The lad shrugged. "I just was not hungry." His fingers plucked languidly at the bed covers.

"Perhaps I have kept you too close." Barry pondered her stepson's steadily growing lethargy.

The housekeeper knocked lightly on the door. "Mr. Looten has arrived, my lady."

"Thank you," Barry answered. "I must go now." She brushed Patrick's forehead lightly with a kiss.

Patrick frowned at her. "Who is this Looten fellow?"

"A very proper gentleman," she said to him. "Sleep well." Barry left him and went down.

Turning from Glenna, Looten released his hold on Pamela's hand. His form-fitting breeches and satin jacket showed his own form to perfection. Expertly flipping the lace on his cuff, he bowed. "Good evening, my lady."

"Can we leave for the theater now?" Pamela asked impatiently.

Glenna rose gracefully from the settee, her gown a brilliant red satin gleaming in the lamplight. "Of course."

"Fortune," Looten said, "smiles sweetly to allow me to escort the three most beautiful women in Bath."

"Why thank you, Mr. Looten," Glenna said, stepping past him. "I do hope it does not prove too great a strain," she murmured as she left the salon.

Getting the ladies settled in the closed carriage was not achieved without difficulty. The fine figure of Mr. Looten was concealed by hooped finery during the short drive to the theater. The building was close to the Pump Room in the basement of Simpson's Assembly Rooms where dances were held weekly.

They had been inside the theater a short time when Pamela whispered, "Look. Prideau."

Glenna's restraining hand kept her from pointing him out.

A young soldier moved hopefully in front of Pamela. "Miss Gromley, may I join you?"

A smile curved her lips. "Why good evening, Lieutenant Horne." She introduced the young army officer to her stepmother and Mr. Looten. "And my lord, what a surprise to see you here," she said when Prideau took a seat behind them. "This is Lieutenant Horne whom I spoke of this morning."

Prideau greeted Horne. "Be at your ease. The army commands neither of us at the moment."

Lieutenant Horne put out his hand. "General Wolfe's death was an unhappy occurrence. I was in that terrible battle."

Prideau shook his hand. "We were fortunate to be victorious after the loss of so able a leader."

"Gentlemen, do not speak of so dour a subject as war," Glenna said.

"Yes, who wishes to hear of such matters," Pamela agreed petulantly, her gown having not yet received a compliment.

Prideau's features lightened. "My cousin, Lady Agatha, bid me to give you her greetings, Mrs. McDowell."

"It is Glenna," she said. "Bath is no place for formality."

"Glenna." He smiled, his eyes moving to Barry and back. "To please you."

"Bid your cousin well for me. She is a kind soul."

"A kind soul? Perhaps," he said, smiling.

Pamela interrupted, "My lord, have you ever seen tonight's play?"

"I do not know what is to be seen," he answered.

"It is *The Beaux' Stratagem*," said. "Quite proper for Bath, would you not agree?"

"There are those in Bath who have no schemes," Horne said, "who go about their affairs honestly and openly."

Glenna could not resist a laugh. " 'Affairs' are neither honest nor open."

"Surely you are not so childish," Pamela said to Horne. "Even I know that each has his or her own ploy."

A tinge of red came to the young man's face, erasing the smile at Glenna's jest. "Do you count yourself among them?"

Panic welled in the young lady's eyes. She liked Horne and did not know how to respond.

Attempting to rescue her, Barry said, "My step-daughter merely means that all of us contrive something at one time or another. Such as a lady who delays her arrival at the theater to be assured a proper audience for her entrance."

"I see," he said.

"There are those who contrive at far deeper schemes." Prideau's deep voice, though low, drew all eyes of the small group to him. He looked at Barry.

Anger met his comment. "There are those who have reason to know *that* truth," Barry returned.

Relief filled Glenna as the curtains rose on the comedy of beaux in Bath. "The play is about to begin," she said.

Between the two acts the audience was entertained with an interlude of oboe and violin music that could hardly be heard above the conversations. Prideau used this opportunity to converse with Glenna and Pamela, despite Horne's and Looten's dark looks. When the curtain fell for the last time, the two gentlemen joined the party for a stroll on the North Parade.

Looten laid his hand over Barry's. He drew her farther ahead of the others. "Can I be of help? You appear troubled."

Barry forced a smile. "I was thinking of my stepson. Bath seems to have had the opposite effect on him than it should have. But forgive me, I bore you with family details."

"You could never do that." Looten tightened his hold.

Barry blushed despite herself. "Why Mr. Looten," she said, glancing back. "I fear we tread too quickly for the others. We must wait for them."

"They do not care," he answered.

"Mr. Looten," she reprimanded.

His features darkened at her tone. He forced himself to relax and smile. He looked to the approaching two pairs and slowly removed his arm. Looten smiled inwardly at Pamela's frown and knew he could convince her that Lady Gromley was trying to attach him so she could add the Loft to her holdings.

Barry, about to reproach him further, saw Prideau's head bent to Pamela's. The girl laughed lightly at something he said and Barry remained silent.

"There you are, Barry," Glenna said, approaching them. "We feared you would become lost."

"One can hardly do that with this full moon," Barry replied. "We are as easily seen as—as that castle." She pointed to the cream-colored turrets rising across the river above Bathampton Downs.

"It is a rule of Bath that one may not play favorites," Glenna said. "Lieutenant Horne, you shall walk with Miss Gromley and you, Mr. Looten, may have my arm." She took his before he could object.

The young officer took advantage immediately. Looten hesitated but did Glenna's bidding and followed her, leaving Prideau and Barry confronting one another uncertainly.

After a long moment Prideau said scathingly, "The castle you see there is Allen's Folly, a sham. But shams are not dangerous once they are known. Your arm, my lady?"

Biting down the desire to snub him, Barry laid her hand lightly on his arm. She drew her breath in sharply when Prideau took her hand and raised it to his lips in a mocking salute before leading her toward the others.

Pondering his actions and words, she walked with him a short way before daring glance. She saw the same mixture of anger and bitterness but something indefinable as well. *It makes no sense*, she thought. *It is I who was wronged.*

Looten waited for them at the end of the Parade and smiled when he saw the iciness between the pair. "I have sent for my coach," he said, ignoring Prideau.

Pamela came to her stepmother's side. "Lieutenant Horne has an excellent scheme for tomorrow."

The young man followed, his expression uneasy, for he had hoped to keep the venture from Prideau's ears, assuming he was interested in Pamela. "Miss Gromley tells me she has not gone through the Abbey Church or walked in the Orange Grove. May I escort her there tomorrow afternoon?"

"What a splendid idea," Glenna said. "It will be so much fun to make a party of it." Her enthusiasm bubbled over. "Delightful! We can even pack a picnic."

Lieutenant Horne smiled.

"An interesting diversion," Prideau said, smiling at Glenna.

She fluttered her fan, moving to his side. "Indeed."

"Are you free, Mr. Looten?" Pamela asked.

"For you, of course." He bowed. "Ah, here is my coach." Looten took her arm.

"We shall see you gentlemen at one then," Glenna told Prideau and Horne. "You know our residence in Queen's Square?" She smiled at their answering nods. "Good evening," she said, allowing Prideau to hand her into the coach.

After the coach's departure Lieutenant Horne stood awkwardly beside Prideau.

"I know an inn," the older man said, taking his arm, "that serves fine refreshment. Would you join me?"

Surprise at the offer clearly showed in Horne's pause. "Of course," he answered, pushing Pamela from his mind. "Is it true Montcalm had seven batteries he failed to employ?"

Looten continued to hold Pamela's hand outside the door in Queen Square. Glenna and Barry bid the gentleman farewell. He kissed Pamela's hand. "A most enjoyable evening."

"I—I too found it entertaining." Pamela drew back her hand as Barry and Glenna entered the house but only succeeded in having Looten step closer.

"Despite your stepmother's unwanted attention. This is but first of many," he said, his voice deepening. He reached to draw her into his arms.

"Pamela, come," Barry called from inside. "It is Patrick!"

"Go at once," Looten said. "I shall call before twelve on the morrow."

Pamela nodded vaguely and hurried inside.

"I am so glad you have returned, my lady," the

housekeeper said when Barry reached the top of the stairs.

"What is it?"

"Tabu, the page, is with him now and he—oh, the poor lad, he's resting peaceably but I thought you should know."

"Tell me what happened," Barry said calmly, despite the cold chill creeping up her spine.

"It was but a short while after you left. Lord Patrick was reading to Tabu," the woman began nervously, "when he became violently ill. Convulsions of some sort from what the page told me, and then he cast up his accounts repeatedly, the poor lamb."

"Why was a physician not summoned?"

"It was all over as quickly as it begun. By the time I reached the bedchamber the worst was past. Lord Patrick was breathing hard and looking very ill, but he insisted I do nothing more than set the bed to rights. After that he appeared near normal."

"I shall see for myself." Barry hurried down the corridor and quietly entered Patrick's room.

"He sleeps," Tabu whispered. "I shall stay with him."

After examining her stepson's features, she nodded. "Thank you, Tabu." Back in the hallway Barry found Glenna and Pamela awaiting her. "He appears well enough," she told them. "But in the morning I shall summon a physician. Let us go to bed. It has been a tiring evening."

A short while later, Barry sat in her chamber in an overstuffed chair facing the window overlooking the street. Patrick. Prideau. Each of them vied for her attention. She had not forgotten the riding "accident" and its implications and still fretted about Prideau's appearance on the estate so soon after it. Her hands went to her throbbing temples. Rising, Barry paced agitatedly, then fell on her bed and wept until she fell asleep.

Much later that evening at the White Hart, after the battles of Quebec and Niagara had been refought to the last detail, Prideau and Horne grew subdued.

"Lost many friends," the younger man said.

"Friends? Never had many," Prideau said.

Horne focused his eyes on the companion he had come to greatly admire during the evening. "That's a shame."

"Took to my books, rather than to play," Prideau said. "Perhaps I made an error," he added quietly.

"Not you, my lord," Horne said, the other's troubled spirit touching him.

"Ever love someone?" Prideau asked, casually.

"Yes, many times," the young man grinned, but Prideau's gravity sobered him. "Perhaps one more seriously of late."

"And have you ever hated?"

"The French to be sure."

"No, I mean someone of the 'gentler' sex," Prideau said.

Horne searched for an answer. "No," he said at last. "Though I've been fair well-angered at times."

"I know a man who hates a woman and yet every time he comes near her, he finds his heart trembling." Prideau spoke lowly, his deep voice vibrating with emotion.

"I do not envy the man." Horne filled his glass. "It is hard enough to wrestle with love," he said, Prideau's mood bringing his own unhappy reflections to mind. "Perhaps if he would examine it closely he would see it is but love he can not admit?" He shrugged, then rose. "Can I see you to your lodgings, my lord?"

"No, I shall stay for a time," Prideau answered. "I thank you for the—company."

"It was my pleasure." The young man walked away.

Alone, Prideau's returned to an early musing. *Why is every thought of* her? He straightened in his chair. *It needs but more discipline.*

And what of your revenge? The question mocked him with the realization that his attempt at revenge could hurt him more than Barry.

Leave Bath. Never see her again, Prideau thought. *Yes*! But then, he immediately weakened. *The excursion to the Abbey—it would not be courteous to cry off.*

What a paltry reason, his thoughts continued to mock him.

On the other hand, Mrs. McDowell will be there, he reasoned. *Beautiful and wealthy enough not to need my money. Perhaps she could be the potion needed to destroy Barry's spell.*

"Damn," Prideau swore aloud, heaving to his feet. He strode angrily into the street. Would the pain never pass? His calm reason and certainty of action were no more, overset by a chance encounter.

I look for Barry wherever I go, damning myself and yet helpless. What is compelling me to be near her? Hate? How could hate make me tremble?

The turmoil within him was so great that Prideau strode on, mindless of all else. Before he realized the distance covered he was in Queen Square staring at Barry's lodgings.

"God help me," he said, feeling completely spent. His shoulders sagged. *Is it hatred? Or love, as Horne suggested*?

Closing his mind to the answer, he drove Barry from his mind, making his way to his lodgings, not realizing how close to the truth, to surrendering his heart he had come.

Chapter Eight

"The lad seems fit enough," the physician announced after entering the salon where the three ladies waited for him.

Pamela turned eagerly to Barry. "Then we may still go on our outing?" Her stepmother's quelling look silenced her.

"What caused so violent an episode?" Barry asked.

"It is difficult to say. I left a packet of James Powders for him. It is to be given four times a day. Also give the lad only soft foods for a few days," he told her.

"You are certain it is nothing serious?" Barry persisted.

"You are overly concerned, my lady," the physician said. "Your stepson is a bit weak and that is mainly due to the restrictions he has been under. He needs fresh air, activity."

"Would it be wise to take him on an outing to the Abbey this afternoon?" she asked.

"It would be just the thing." He nodded. "And for you also. You look a bit worn. Take care or I shall have you as a patient," the physician said.

"I think not." She forced a smile. "Thank you."

"Don't fret over the lad," he repeated. "Good day." He nodded to all as he took his leave.

Glenna patted her arm. "I'm certain he is right."

"Yes," Barry said. "I shall tell Patrick he is to go with us to the Abbey."

"But the gentlemen are to call for *us*," Pamela said in protest. She grew sullen beneath the reproving stares of the older women. "There isn't much beyond an hour to dress," she said weakly.

Barry sighed, shaking her head.

"Then let us begin." Glenna took the young woman's arm, unable to decide whether to laugh or scold.

Despite the protested lack of time, Pamela was ready and primly seated in the Green Salon looking very fetching in a pink India cotton frock with large red bows at the sleeves and in the center of the hooped skirt.

"Mr. Looten," the butler announced the first caller.

The gentleman bowed before her. "How charming you look today, Miss Gromley."

"Thank you, sir," Pamela responded warmly to his admiring glance. *How handsome he is*, she thought, *but so is Lieutenant Horne*. She collected her wits, realizing he was looking expectantly at her. "Yes?"

"I was wondering when Lady Gromley would join us?"

"Mrs. McDowell and my stepmother should be down shortly." She paused. "My brother, Patrick, suffered some childhood affliction last evening and set the entire household awry," Pamela said. "The physician pronounced him well this morning and he is to go with us." She ended with a distressed sigh.

"What a trying experience for you," Looten said, taking hold of her hand. "A beautiful young woman such as yourself should never be so troubled." He laid a kiss upon her wrist. "I have told you that before," he said.

Glenna paused unseen in the doorway, contemplating Pamela's guilty blush and the gentleman's complete ease. "Mr. Looten, how prompt you are."

Looten straightened. "With several hours in the company of three beautiful ladies beckoning, I could do little but pace until the appointed hour arrived." He bowed, then led her to the settee.

"Lord Prideau," the butler announced. "Lieutenant Horne."

"Good morning, Glenna," Prideau greeted her as he kissed her hand. "Miss Gromley." He bowed while Horne fretfully awaited his opening. "You are both beautiful this morning," he said before sauntering to the fireplace and leaning against the mantel.

"Is Lady Gromley not going with us?" Horne asked, maneuvering a seat beside Pamela.

"She will be here," Glenna answered him. "Lord Patrick is to join our party," she informed the gentlemen. "Barry will want him to be with her, so Lieutenant Horne and Pamela shall ride in your carriage, my lord," she told Prideau.

He arched a brow. "And you?"

"With you, of course," she flirted.

Barry hurried into the salon. "Excuse my tardiness, gentlemen." Her faint smile disappeared at the sight of Prideau. "Lord Patrick is ready."

Shaking hands while making light of the splint, Patrick responded to the gentlemen's greetings in good spirits. The ladies were handed into the coaches and the outing began.

In Prideau's coach conversation was lively. Glenna flirted outrageously with both Prideau and Horne, much to Pamela's consternation. The young lady consoled herself by basking in Horne's tongue-tied admiration.

In Looten's coach, however, Patrick had taken a dislike to the gentleman.

"Do you feel ill?" Barry asked, concerned when he refused to be chatted from his sullen mood.

"It is nothing," he mumbled, his ire rising beneath Looten's condescending gaze.

"Are you certain?" Barry put her hand to his forehead. "You do not feel overly warm." She studied him closely.

"I am fine," Patrick insisted, smiling.

"You must stay in the coach if you do not feel well."

"Oh, no. I have read that the Abbey is called the 'Lantern of England.' " Patrick's enthusiasm rose. "It said the nave was lighted by the most huge expanse of windows."

"And we shall see it now," Barry said as the coach drew to a halt.

Pamela straightened her skirt carefully after her first glimpse of the Abbey. "How quaint. Is that Jacob's ladder?"

"No," Patrick corrected her with enraging sweetness. "It is what a bishop thought he saw in a vision."

Laughing aside her brother's words, the young lady placed a hand on Looten's arm. Pamela brightened visibly at Lieutenant Horne's reaction.

Patrick pointed to a solemn monument at one side of the nave. "What is that?"

"It is a bishop, lying in prayerful repose," Glenna

told him, following Looten and Barry into the interior of the church.

The leaded windows comprising the whole of the western edge filled the church with hallowed light. Barry's eyes widened with pleasure at the intricate, delicate fan revolving above. She looked behind her. Her eyes met Prideau's. For a second both forgot the past and shared their response to the beauty above them.

"Trusty devils, the monks," Horne said, noting the locked offering box.

Prideau stiffened, dropped a mask over his feelings and looked away.

Barry felt bereft and moved nearer to Glenna.

Pamela opened *Robert's Guide to Bath* and read. "To our left should be the tracery of a chantry from the sixteenth century."

"Why do you suppose it was made?" Pamela asked, gazing up at the fragile open stonework.

"Whoever gave the endowment for the singing of the Masses wished there to be a public record of it," Barry answered. "Perhaps he rested easier for it."

"There are those who should feel a special need for prayers," Prideau's voice cut in coldly.

Patrick glanced from Prideau to his stepmother and moved between then. "Can we see the Saxon cross? It is at the far end of the Abbey, near the Roman ruins," he told them. At Prideau's nod Patrick led them to the cross. He begged to be allowed to wander through the tombstones in the cemetery and ran off as soon as permission was given. Glenna followed.

"Can we not stroll in the Orange Grove while Patrick pleases his morbid humor?" Pamela asked.

Horne was at her side in an instant. "I shall be

happy to escort you there," he said. "We should tell Lady Gromley."

"If you insist," she answered as they moved toward her stepmother. She looked at Looten, and smiled at his frown. "Join us," Pamela invited while Horne spoke with Barry.

"Of course," he said, his tone a bit sharp.

"Go on," Barry told Horne. "I will bring Patrick."

Prideau suddenly spoke. "I shall remain with them."

Realizing there was no polite way to prevent him, Barry waved the others away. "We shall come in a few moments. Patrick will tire quickly."

Barry and Prideau stood alone together. "Elysium," she murmured, watching Patrick go from stone to stone, reading the immutable messages, some cut a century before.

"Abode of the blessed," Prideau said behind her.

Several minutes of silence passed. Barry looked for a flash of Patrick's jacket among the tombstones. "I wonder where he could have gone," she said uneasily. "He was not well last evening and this heat—I never should have allowed him to come." She began walking forward.

"What harm can the lad come to?" Prideau inquired, puzzled by the intensity of her concern.

"He had a bout of vomiting last night and the physician could find no reason for it. Patrick has always been extremely healthy but since coming to Bath—"

"So you dote on the boy as much as he on you," Prideau said, his voice edged with sarcasm.

"He is my stepson."

"And you his first love?"

Barry clenched her hands. "You are insulting, my lord."

"If you lost him, I believe it would pain you far

worse than Gromley's death." He watched her scanning the stones. "You *should* know the pain of loss," he said bitterly.

"I know loss." Barry swung around to face him.

A low groan reached their ears, forestalling further words.

"Patrick!" she shouted, dashing forward. Rounding a large stone Barry saw the boy writhing on the ground, clutching his arms to his stomach. "What is it?"

"Do not—know," Patrick choked out. Beads of perspiration were on his forehead; his face was contorted in pain.

Prideau went down on one knee opposite Barry. "Let me take the lad. Horne can fetch the physician while my coach carries him to your lodgings."

"Yes, but quickly." She rose, watching Prideau scoop Patrick up in his arms. His strong, lengthy strides caused her to half-run to keep pace.

"Patrick has had another attack," she called to the three standing near the coach. "Where is Mr. Looten?"

"We do not know," Pamela replied, going to Patrick's side.

"Someone must go for the physician," Prideau said. "Lieutenant Horne, take Mr. Looten's coach and fetch him to our lodgings. He is on Westgate. Do you know the direction?"

"Yes."

"Hurry. Tell him it is urgent. I shall explain to Mr. Looten. He cannot object."

Reaching Queen Street, Prideau reined his blowing team to a heavy-handed halt before Barry's lodgings. He leaped down, took Patrick, and was through the door, brushing past the butler, before Barry and Pamela had tumbled from the coach.

"See to Lord Prideau when he comes down," Barry instructed her stepdaughter without pausing. She lifted her skirts and took the steps two at a time. She entered his room to find the housekeeper and Prideau hurriedly removing Patrick's jacket while Tabu, Glenna's page, hovered behind them.

The housekeeper held a washbasin out for the boy. When the bout passed, Patrick's features eased somewhat, and Prideau gently laid him back against the pillows.

Motioning for the bowl to be taken away, Barry wiped her stepson's face with a cool, damp cloth.

Patrick raised his hand, attempting a weak smile.

"The physician will be here soon," she said, trying to summon a smile.

"I am—sorry—to have ruined—your—"

"Hush." Barry put a finger to his lips. "Rest."

He nodded as she loosened and removed his cravat.

"Watch him closely," Barry instructed the housekeeper. "Call me at once if there is any change."

Prideau followed Barry into the corridor.

"Back to your duties," she ordered the staff gathered in the hall and Prideau's stern expression hastened them away.

The sleepless nights, the strain of the past months weighed heavily on Barry. She raised large careworn eyes to Prideau's. "I thank you for your prompt action," she said with heart-tugging gratitude. "Pamela will have some refreshment for you."

The desire to comfort her rose above all others. "Barry—" Prideau said, reaching to caress her cheek.

She stepped away from his touch. "You have made

your feelings for me quite clear—in the past and now. Thank you for your help," she said, not realizing her action hit him harder than any hand. "Excuse me." Her chin rose and she walked away.

Chapter Nine

"I fail to see why we must remain at home simply because Patrick has the colic," Pamela grumbled over her needlework in the salon that evening.

"Your brother is seriously ill," Barry told her. "The physician said he may still be in danger if we cannot find the cause of these attacks." She dropped a stitch, biting her lip, then laid aside the breeches she was knitting for her stepson.

The butler entered and addressed Barry. "Mr. Looten desires to know if you will receive him, my lady."

Dismay filled her, overflowing into her features.

Glenna rose. "I shall speak to him, Barry. You look quite worn out. Why don't you look in on Patrick and then retire."

"Yes, I shall." Barry smiled gratefully as she rose. "Good evening." She nodded to both and quickly left the salon.

"Couldn't we entertain Mr. Looten for a short while?" Pamela asked. "He is such a—a genteel person."

"Show the gentleman to us," Glenna ordered.

"Mrs. McDowell. Miss Gromley." The powdered,

patched, and scented gentleman greeted then effu-
sively, taking Pamela's hand. "How does Lord Patrick
get on? I could not bear the pleasures of Simpson's
Assembly Rooms knowing how upset you must be."
His eyes swung to Glenna. "And Lady Gromley?

"She has retired early," Glenna answered coolly.

Looten's attention turned to the younger woman.
"What a comfort you must be to her. Any but you
would have gone into hysterics." His tone caressed her
vanity.

"You are too kind," Pamela said, blushing.

"Forgive me, Mr. Looten. It has been a long day."
Glenna rose, indicating he should leave.

"Yes, yes." He sprang lightly to his feet. "I shall
call on the morrow. Until then, Miss Gromley." He
raised her hand to his lips. "Mrs. McDowell." He
bowed and gave a smiling nod which did little to melt
the iciness he read in her eyes, very different from the
trust in Pamela's.

Glenna swooped into Barry's bedchamber. "Why
are you not asleep? Tabu will call you if Patrick wors-
ens," she said, standing beside the bed.

"I know," Barry answered. "Your page is hardly
older than Patrick and so—so great a help."

"Yes, I shall dislike losing him," Glenna said, sitting upon the bed.

"But why? He seems perfectly devoted to you."

"He shall be far happier doing—something else."
Regret flickered in her voice. Suddenly seriousness
flared. "Mr. Looten however—Pamela has been taken
in by his well-turned calves."

"Do I detect dislike?" Barry asked in surprise. "He
has been a gentleman."

"I think not." Glenna lowered her voice. "Looten

plays a close game, spouting sonnets of concern for you and whispering in Pamela's ear at each chance. I cannot like it."

"But—"

"And the girl is interested."

Barry shook her head. "Mr. Looten may not be perfect but she is also interested in Lieutenant Horne."

"And Prideau has shown enough interest in me," Glenna continued. "Mr. Looten believes he has no real competition."

Barry raised a startled gaze. "That—is—true."

"Be warned. Looten is not to be trusted."

Barry's anger flared unaccountably. "Pamela may need forewarning but I do not." She reached out. "I am sorry. I know it is but my interest that prompts your words."

Rising, Glenna patted Barry's hand. "I bid you good night." She paused at the door but her friend's thoughts were already far away and she slipped out.

Barry beat down the sob that threatened her. *Oh, the wretched, wretched man*, she thought, closing her misting eyes against Prideau's image. *I love him still. What am I to do?*

There is nothing you can do, came the unwelcome answer. *He puzzlingly holds you in disgust.*

Barry tried to deny this but could not. *He has shown desire but then his bitterness comes through. And*, she sighed, *he would be an excellent match for Glenna.*

A vision of the promise rose, given so long ago, appeared vividly before her, and tears crept down Barry's cheeks.

"Patrick is much improved this past week," Glenna told Barry, removing a gown from her friend's wardrobe. "You *are* going to attend the weekly assembly at Simpson's Rooms with Pamela and me." An iron determination lay beneath her chatter.

"But he is still so listless. Even having his arm pronounced healed did not cheer him."

"Tabu shall stay with him," Glenna said.

"But he is only a lad. I do not think—"

"You will find no one better to watch Patrick," Glenna said adamantly. "Ever since I took Tabu from a master who beat him and scarcely bothered to feed him, he has had the inordinate wish to please me. Not only does he realize your stepson's safety is important to me, but he has a growing fondness for Patrick." Glenna suddenly clapped her hands in inspiration. "Would it not be perfect if Tabu were to become Patrick's valet? He would be happier in a man's world than in mine.

"But," Glenna said, quelling Barry's hope that she had forgotten her original purpose, "we shall speak of this later. This evening *you* are my concern. I should have insisted earlier that you continue to go out with us." Seeing her words had no effect she continued. "Think of your duty to Pamela. She is driving poor Horne to distraction. Now off with that dress or I shall remove it." Glenna tapped her foot threateningly. "The butler always does my bidding, no matter what it may be," she warned pointedly when the other did not move. "Shall I call him?" She took a step towards the door.

"Oh, very well," Barry conceded. "But I mean to take Patrick to Gromley Hall next week."

Glenna raised a brow. "Never say you mean to leave Pamela in my care?"

"No, she shall return with me no matter what the protests," Barry answered. She stepped out of her day gown. "You shall have Prideau to yourself."

"An intriguing idea," Glenna said, watching her closely.

"Be certain before you give your heart," Barry warned.

"Ah, but remember, marriage is best when your affections are not engaged," Glenna answered. "Let me fasten your stays more tightly."

Stepping into the Assembly Room's main ballroom, Prideau's eye fell on the three ladies who also had just entered. *How worn Barry looks*, he thought. His lips compressed into a thin line at the sight of Looten standing close beside her. He forced his gaze to Glenna and appreciatively studied the effect of her sea-blue satin gown.

Catching Prideau's eyes upon her, Glenna fluttered her fan invitingly. "Good evening, my lord," she greeted him warmly when he had strolled to her side.

"You are in splendid looks this evening." Prideau bowed. He gave a nod to Horne, who was bearing down on the group before turning to Barry. "Lord Patrick?"

"Improving," she answered, and would have stepped away had not Glenna's hand stayed her.

"Prideau, they are assembling for the minuets. Would you consent to lead me?" she asked him.

He smiled. "It would be my pleasure."

"And of course you must dance with Barry first," Glenna told him, taking the advantage of one of Beau Nash's decrees that minuets were to be danced in order of social precedence, each gentleman leading the ladies in order of their rank. "Ah, there is but one couple before you. I shall return." She fluttered away.

"My lord, I am not accustomed to dancing. If you prefer—" Barry began to say.

"There is a rule that none may leave the line once they take their place," Prideau replied stiffly, glad for it.

Barry raised troubled eyes to his. "It was good of you to send the cakes to Patrick. He is enjoying them." She watched his smile play across his features.

"I am glad to hear he improves. Perhaps he shall yet get to see the sites of Bath."

"There shall be no opportunity for that. We are to leave Bath shortly." Barry looked at the pair dancing the minuet, their powdered locks silver in the chandeliers' light.

"I had heard no mention of this," Prideau said slowly. He saw her glance and fell silent.

As they waited the realization came to Barry that this was probably the last time she would ever see Prideau since they were leaving Bath. She followed him onto the floor and moved through the steps of the minuet in a daze.

Prideau felt the intensity of her gaze and met it, closing his mind to the denials of reason, his emotion bittersweet.

At the far side Pamela watched the two.

"They make a handsome pair," Lieutenant Horne noted, following her glare. "It is plain to see how the matter lies with them."

The young lady turned to him with cold hauteur. "What nonsense are you spouting? They detest one another. They are dancing now only because of Mrs. McDowell's prank."

"Hardly." He laughed softly, more certain of Prideau's feelings than the man was himself.

"I wish you would not be so childish," Pamela said.

"It is you who should know I am not being so."

"Your meaning, sir?"

"It is you who have been infantile, fawning outrageously over Looten and using me as your ploy." Horne threw aside the caution he had chaffed under. "You may regret it."

Looten appeared. "Miss Gromley, you are distressed?"

"A gentleman at last." She spoke scathingly and turned from Horne, laying her hand upon the other's arm.

"Perhaps you would like some refreshment?" Looten asked, leading her away. "Your stepmother appears to be enjoying herself," he commented.

"Yes," Pamela replied, glancing back at Horne.

Looten sighed dramatically. He looked about and then said. "She sees she has failed with me and has even more reason for being rid of Patrick."

Pamela blanched. "Surely you err," she protested.

"There is so much you do not know," Looten said bitterly. "Has Lord Patrick not had too many 'accidents?' "

"Lord James, our guardian, said I was not to be concerned," Pamela said nervously.

"He is in her clutches as I said." Looten paused. "My dear Pamela." His sympathy eased her as much as his manner charmed. *Yes*, he thought, seeing the answering glow in her eyes. *This simpering girl believes everything I tell her.*

With the music's end, Prideau escorted Barry from the floor. Informed by the Master of the Dance that Mrs. McDowell had sent her apologies, he nodded for the following couple to take their place and offered his arm to Barry. Compelled by an inexplicable force, Prideau asked, "A brief stroll outdoors?"

Barry's heart made her reply, "If you wish, my

lord." Outside the cool evening air did little to dispel her sudden warmth.

Prideau knew not what he meant to do, to say, only that he wanted to lengthen their time together. "It has been many years since we walked alone—Barry."

Barry's heart somersaulted. Did she dare hope? Her eyes flew to his but found them unfathomable.

"Neither of us is the foolish youth we were twelve years past," Prideau continued, leading her into the shadows of the colonnade. His bitterness broke through. "We both have learned the value of many things."

"I cannot make out your meaning. Why do you harbor such coldness for me?" Barry asked, turning to him.

Prideau's hands gripped her arms. "It is not cold I feel for you, by God," he swore, his voice breaking. He vowed to stride away but his hands went to her shoulders.

Barry was startled by his fierce tone. "What is it you want of me?" she cried.

"There is nothing I would not have done for you," Prideau said heavily.

"Nor I for you." Her voice broke on the last word.

Prideau reached up and caressed her cheek, then drew her gently to him.

Slowly Barry's arms crept around his neck. She leaned against him.

Suddenly Prideau thrust her back, his anger sharp and clear. "No," he said. "No," he repeated to himself. "I will be a fool only once." Turning sharply, he stalked away.

Barry sank against the column. *Fool*, echoed in her mind. *I am the greater one.*

* * *

"There you are, Prideau," Glenna greeted him coyly outside the doors of the Assembly Rooms. She pursed her lips, studying his black look. "Come, let us walk. I must look for Barry. I was told she stepped out for a time but has not returned." His arm stiffened beneath her hand and his features darkened further. She guided him towards the half-empty Parades. "Tell me what has upset you. Do not glower." Glenna tapped his shoulder lightly with her fan.

Prideau sought to regain control of his emotions. "You have not spoken of your life since we last met. Tell me of it."

Sensing something was very awry and knowing he had gone out with Barry, Glenna began to chatter, recalling all the amusing incidents she could. When his features lightened she ended, "So you see, my life is not sadly wanting."

"Did you spend all of the last twelve years in America?"

"No. I was home for a brief time before my father died. It was not a happy time—for many reasons."

She recalled the abandoned betrothal. "Life's twists are often not pleasant," she said. "Barry's life is ample evidence of that."

"She does not have the look of one whom life has been unkind to," Prideau returned bitterly.

"What? Robed in *my* gowns. I would forswear her if she did," Glenna said. "Don't let her fine clothes or her manner fool you," she continued. "Pride alone supports her bearing. Gromley was a compulsive gambler. His lands are being sold to cover debts. Even his country seat may be lost."

"Why tell me this? It is not my concern." Prideau looked away from her admonishing gaze.

"I had not seen or heard from Barry for six years

when I saw her in London this February past," Glenna said slowly. "If only you knew how distressed she was for her stepchildren." Her hand gripped his arm. "She has not a care for herself."

"I do not believe you."

"Three years ago she was forced to choose between Gromley and a niggardly harridan of a cousin who was making her life a living hell. Perhaps you would have preferred her to be a White Chapel 'lady'—or to nobly starve?"

"This is none of my affair," Prideau repeated, anger rising at the further complications this news added to his turmoil.

"Is it not?" Glenna posed the question softly. "Perhaps you had best seek out your former secretary—more your father's than yours from what your cousin Lady Agatha tells me. Hawks, wasn't it? It could be he can tell you something to indicate Barry should still be very much your concern."

Prideau removed her hand from his arm and walked away. He did not pause, did not trust himself to hear more, lest all reason be lost.

Chapter Ten

Barry paced outside Patrick's door two days later. "He cannot endure any more of these convulsions."

"Come to the salon," Glenna said. "You shall fret yourself into an attack." She took her friend's hand and gently led her towards the stairs. "The physician will manage. You can be of no aid standing out here."

The truth of the argument convinced Barry to concede. Arriving in the salon, she paced for a time, then sat. Picking up her knitting, she asked distractedly, "Where is Pamela?"

"I believe she went to the lending library. The maid has gone with her." Glenna paged through the *Gazette*.

"Pamela has maintained her cheerfulness well in the face of Lieutenant Horne's abandonment," Barry said.

"Yes, and developed a remarkable appetite for reading of late," Glenna said dryly. "And Prideau seems to have lost interest in calling, but then I fear he has been offended," she said, broaching a subject that has been anathema.

A soft blush rose to Barry's cheeks. She grimaced and plied her needles with renewed determination and she grimaced. "I explained it all to you the morning after the ball."

"But never said what really happened," Glenna said.

"Men are not to be understood," Barry said curtly, her brows deeply furrowed.

Pamela strode into the salon, her color heightened, her breath rushed. "Why is the physician's carriage here?"

"Patrick has been stricken again," Barry said worriedly. At sight of the physician, she dropped her knitting, rising.

"Miss Gromley. Mrs. McDowell," he greeted the ladies. "I must speak with you alone, Lady Gromley."

His somber visage contracted her heart. "There is nothing that these two may not hear," she said.

"Alone, my lady. It is best," he insisted.

Glenna moved gracefully from the salon with a reassuring nod. "I shall see if I can be of assistance upstairs."

"You mean to speak about my brother," Pamela said adamantly, and took a seat.

Her icy tone, unheard since coming to Bath, penetrated Barry's distress. "Speak freely, sir," she said, looking at Pamela.

The portly physician adjusted the wide cuff of his frock coat, then fidgeted with the lace on his sleeve.

A vise gripped Barry's heart. "My stepson shall not die?"

"He is weak," he began, choosing his words carefully. "Tell me, my lady, had he been given any food other than what your cook has prepared?"

"I believe not," she answered.

"And all of you partake of this food?"

"Of course. What is your meaning?"

"I am certain someone is poisoning the lad."

Gasps escaped both women. Barry blanched. Confirmation flickered across Pamela's features.

"Can you be certain?" Barry asked fearfully.

"Not absolutely, but there is much that indicates it. I recall reading of a Shropshire man who was fed a small dose of poison each day. The physicians were mystified by his spells which were much like Lord Patrick's. His wife was made to confess when caught in the act of putting the poison in his bread."

"Why did the man not die at once?" Pamela asked.

"Not enough was given to kill, but it remains in the body and when sufficient becomes present—the attacks." He shrugged. "The victim becomes progressively weaker, refuses to eat, and will die if the offensive material is not removed from his diet. Lord Patrick may not survive another attack."

Pamela turned to her stepmother, her voice trembling. "You mean to kill him! Father's death is not enough."

"Miss Gromley!" The physician stepped towards her, alarmed by the outburst.

"Ask her. Ask her about Patrick's riding 'accident.' " The young lady's voice rose. "Ask who insisted we come to Bath."

"Pamela." Barry rose and went to her.

"No." Her stepdaughter slapped away the proffered hand. "I will not permit it. Do you not see?" She turned wide eyes to the physician. "When it is done she shall turn on me."

"You have been reading too many novels," Barry rebuked her.

Hurrying back into the salon, Glenna asked, "Why are you shouting?"

"She is poisoning Patrick!" Pamela stepped back from the physician, trying to regain her composure. "I will not let you do this," she yelled at Barry and ran from the room.

"A glass of water," the physician ordered, taking hold of Barry's arm. He guided her to the settee and commanded her to drink from the glass Glenna handed her.

"The lad is being poisoned?" Glenna asked.

He nodded.

"Who can be doing it?" Barry raised haunted eyes to both. "Why?"

"The housekeeper spoke of your returning to Gromley Hall at the week's end," he began kindly.

"Yes, I did not like Patrick's continued weakness."

"And Miss Gromley?" he asked.

"Is a highly excitable young lady who would do anything to cause a scene," Glenna told him. "Someone has put the idea in her head that Lady Gromley was responsible for her brother's broken arm. Reading ridiculous novels has added to her too-vivid imagination."

"It was no accident," Barry said hollowly.

"That matter was investigated and it was declared such," Glenna said. "You know me well, sir, and I swear on my honor there is no reason to suspect Lady Gromley of any foul deed. You may as well suspect the maid who carries Lord Patrick's tray to his room."

The physician studied both women closely. "It would be best if you did as planned," he said at last. "The lad is weak, but maybe now the deed is known he will be safe. With good food and country air he shall recover."

"Do not cheer me with falsehoods," Barry said.

"I speak the truth," he said, taking her hand. "I shall leave you some powders to calm Miss Gromley and a potion to give you a good night's sleep. See that they take it," he instructed Glenna.

"I shall. Thank you," she told him gratefully. "Now let me see you out." She took his arm. "Why don't you lie down for a time, Barry? Lord Patrick is resting."

"Yes," Barry answered vaguely, and walked from the morning room lost in thought.

"No need to see me to the door," he said to Glenna. "See to Lady Gromley or you shall have two invalids on your hands. A word of warning. Miss Gromley's words could do much mischief."

Glenna nodded soberly and bid the physician farewell. The plot had become monstrously deep.

Three days' passing saw Patrick much improved, though whether for the plot being laid aside or for the fact that he was given no food that had not been prepared and carried to him by the page Tabu was uncertain.

Pamela changed dramatically after another visit to the lending library the following day. She lapsed into a mysterious silence and now maintained a tight-lipped composure even to the point of not raising objections to the proposed return to Gromley Hall, much to Barry's relief.

"My lady," the butler interrupted Barry as she spoke with the housekeeper about the packing. "Lord Prideau has called asking for Mrs. McDowell."

"Yes?" she asked, seeing no problem in the request.

"Madam has stepped out for a time."

"Have you told him this?"

"Yes, my lady. He wishes to speak with you. I have shown him to the salon."

"Continue as we were," she instructed the house-keeper. "I shall return in a few moments."

Her quick steps slowed outside the salon's door. Taking a deep breath, she strode in. "Yes, my lord?"

Prideau took in her worn countenance; saw how thin she was becoming. "I learned Lord Patrick has taken a turn for the worse," he said, carefully to hide the tumult of his feelings.

"He is much improved." Barry clasped her hands before her. "Thank you for your concern." Saying those words reminded her of the cakes he had sent Patrick. Fear showed momentarily in her eyes. "We are to leave later this week," she told him.

"You'll return to Gromley Hall?"

"Glenna is to remain in Bath," she parried.

"And Pamela?"

"I did not realize your affections had been engaged by my stepdaughter," she said coldly.

"And if they have?" Prideau asked with equal stiff-ness, the conversation going far astray from what he had intended.

"Then absence shall be a proving ground. We know your loyalty, after all, do we not?" The words were out before she could halt them.

Prideau was puzzled by her words, at the pained edge to her tone. Glenna's admonition that "pride alone" sustained her came to mind. He sought a reason to stay. "May I see the lad?"

"You have done quite enough." Barry spoke with carefully controlled words. "I am extremely busy packing. You must excuse me." She turned away.

He grasped at any reason to stay with her. "When may I call upon Mrs. McDowell?"

"You may call this evening," Barry answered, her

back to him. She walked away quickly, half running to the stairs after she had gained the corridor.

For several moments Prideau stared at the open door. He had come to apologize. Honesty had compelled him to admit Barry had not goaded his behavior towards her the night of the ball. Glenna's words had added to his discomfort, which grew each day, inducing him to call.

The possibility of his being in error about Barry haunted his thoughts, adding an ever-heavier weight to his distress. His mind assured him he was right; his heart entreated her forgiveness. Now she was going away.

It is best, Prideau told himself. *What is being said about her and the lad is no concern of mine.* He strode from the salon, knowing in his heart her evident anguish was weakening his resolve.

His steps echoed to the upper story where Barry stood, her white-knuckled hands gripping the banister. *I cannot be correct*, she told herself again. *I cannot. He would never do so wicked a deed.*

But he had spoken of revenge. Worse, that she should suffer a loss. Most condemning, his was the only outside food her stepson had been given. Barry suddenly felt light-headed.

Glenna looked up the stairs at her friend's frozen stance. She raised her candy-striped skirt and quickly pattered towards her. "Has Patrick taken ill again?"

"Was Prideau in London after I left you?" Barry asked.

"No, he left soon after you did," Glenna answered. "Why do you ask? Was it his carriage I saw driving away?"

Barry ignored the questions and released her hold

on the railing, her shoulders sagging. "The packing is almost completed. Prideau is to call on you this evening. You should not see him," Barry said.

"Prideau is a gentleman," Glenna replied.

"You cannot know him." Barry's eyes misted. "You cannot. I do not." She turned and hastened away.

Chapter Eleven

Glenna watched Barry draw on her light traveling cloak. "I wish you would not go."

"Say no more, please," Barry pleaded. The dark circles beneath her eyes emphasized her exhaustion.

"But whoever is trying to harm Patrick may feel freer to act at Gromley Hall."

"I mean to send him to Lord James," she answered.

"Have you told Patrick this?"

"Not yet. When he is better." Barry took hold of Glenna's hands. "It is far too good of you to send Tabu with us. His presence makes me feel easier somehow. How good you have been to us all." Tears welled in Barry's eyes.

"It is you who have amused me," Glenna returned.

"You will send me an accounting of all I owe?" Barry asked.

"As soon as I collect my wits," Glenna replied. "You attend to the shearing of your sheep and I will attend to your account," she said, teasing.

"If I could but believe that." Barry sighed, then impulsively kissed her. "I wish you joy."

Glenna returned the embrace. "And I, you. Will you

not tell me what troubles you so?" Glenna asked a final time.

"Patrick's health, of course."

"Excuse me." The housekeeper stood at the door.

Glenna turned to her. "Yes?"

"The maid has asked if she might go with you, Lady Gromley. She says she will serve in any position you wish."

"I am sorry but that is impossible." Barry said, seeing no way to bear the expense. "Please explain it is no lack on her part. A complete staff awaits our return."

"I shall see to it," the housekeeper assured her. "I bid you a safe journey."

"And I thank you for all you have done during our stay."

The woman blushed pleasurably at such uncommon praise, nodded and withdrew.

"We must be off," Barry said, clasping her hands nervously. "Before we go, however I—I must warn you." She grew agitated. "Warn you of Prideau. No, do not smile. I am not free to speak of all I believe of him, but he is not to be trusted. I—I fear for his mind."

"Whatever can you mean?" Glenna asked. "I spoke with him last evening at the theater and he was most solicitous of Patrick."

This news of his concern confirmed Barry's suspicions. Fear sprang to her eyes. "You did not tell him we were to depart this morning?"

Glenna reached for her hand. "What is it?"

"I can say no more. Beware of him."

"You are merely jealous," Glenna said flippantly, making a last desperate attempt to evoke a confidence.

Barry studied her gloved hands for a moment, then raised her eyes. "I will not deny that, even now, I care for him. But I would never put that in the way of your happiness."

Her simply spoken words struck Glenna's heart.

"There is no chance for mine own, but I fear for you if you seek your happiness with Prideau—and not because of his past perfidy. I beg of you to take care." Barry gave her friend a final embrace.

Despite the pandemonium prevailing in the street, Barry judged the butler was making good work of it. Patrick was safely settled among the pillows in the coach and the last few bandboxes were being tied to the mound of baggage sprouting from its boot.

A heavy step startled her. Relaxing at sight of the young gentleman, Barry smiled. "Lieutenant Horne, good day."

Horne bowed. "And to you, Lady Gromley. Prideau was telling me that Pamela—Miss Gromley is to go with you." He took in the heap of bandboxes being tied down.

"I thought it best," she answered. "It is kind of you to come and bid us farewell. Did Prideau know we were to depart this morning?" she asked nervously.

"I believe not." He paused, diffident. "Miss Gromley—well, she is a troublesome girl for you, I do not doubt," Horne said awkwardly. "But merely young. Not truly a bad sort."

"Most assuredly," Barry agreed with an understanding smile. "Perhaps we shall see you in London next spring?" she asked.

Horne brightened. "By that time I may have attained my promotion." He turned at the rustling of satin in the doorway. Giving Barry a slight bow, he walked towards Pamela who had stopped at the door. "Miss Gromley."

"Lieutenant Horne," she acknowledged him coldly.

"I—I wish to bid you a good journey." He stumbled over his words in the face of her manner.

Barry circumspectly moved to the coach to speak with Patrick.

"You needn't have bothered," Pamela continued haughtily, fully irked by their last encounter since the young man had shown no degree of repentance. "There are those who appreciate my—sensibilities."

Horne studied her closely, awaiting the indication that she was in jest. None came. "I credited you with better sense," he said at last with manly foolishness, the regret for her behavior heavy in his eyes. "But then perhaps you are simply too young to have any."

Stamping her foot angrily, Pamela opened her mouth to retort but choked on the words. Her chin high in the air, she stalked past him to the coach.

A frown creased Barry's features, but she stepped aside and permitted her stepdaughter to enter. "Lieutenant Horne," she said, going to him and giving her hand, "she is, after all, very young. Youth is apt to be imprudent if not handled carefully."

"Have a care for her." He took her hand. "If ever I happen to be near Gromley Hall, may I call?"

"Of course, Lieutenant Horne." Barry smiled, pleased that Pamela had attracted so sincere a young man who was willing to look past her obvious faults.

Horne threw a last beseeching glance at the young lady after handing Barry into the coach, but she steadfastly refused to look his way and he reluctantly closed the door.

Glenna tripped lightly from the house and blew a kiss to the coach. "God speed."

"His blessings on you," Barry returned with heartfelt sincerity and waved as the coach lurched forward.

"Take care." Glenna fluttered her kerchief at Tabu, perched atop the coach.

The small black lad waved his hat, content that no one could see his tears. Torn between sorrow at leaving his mistress and his joy at serving Lord Patrick, he was relieved the decision was not his to make.

In a flutter of kerchiefs the coach disappeared from the square.

"Lieutenant Horne." Glenna smiled at him. "It is not too late for a turn in the Pump Room. Could you be of a mind to escort me?"

"It would be a great honor, madam."

She saw his eyes wander to the end of the square. "I fear it will not be vastly entertaining."

"Yes." Horne sighed, then gave a foolish grin, aware he had been obvious. "But," he said, in an attempt to redeem himself, "it could never be dull with you about, Mrs. McDowell. Perhaps we will chance upon Prideau. He was far too quiet this morning for my liking."

"Let me fetch my parasol," she said rewarding him with a brilliant smile. "Tend to the gentleman," she ordered the butler and fluttered back through the door.

Glenna quickly maneuvered Lieutenant Horne to the front of the Pump Room. "Prideau, good morning," she greeted with a beguiling smile and a languid curtsy.

Prideau insolently slapped his snuffbox shut. "Mrs. McDowell. Lieutenant Horne."

"Bother, the waters have not cured him of his bile." She fluttered her fan lightly, leaning on Horne's arm.

A tight-lipped smile rewarded her sally.

"Better, my lord," Glenna said airily. She poised a hand on her forehead. "I am bereft, gentlemen."

"But what is wrong?" Lieutenant Horne straightened as if run through by a dagger.

Prideau viewed her pose more placidly. "Shall we step apart?" he suggested. "Come along, Horne." Prideau smiled at the young man's confusion. "It shall be made clear soon enough."

"You are piqued." Glenna's chin rose haughtily, but her prattle continued as the three strolled from the Pump Room. Fluttering her fan prettily in greeting to those they passed, she led on until they were alone.

"You have heard the insinuations regarding Barry and her stepson," Glenna began. "I fear for the boy's life as well as her own." She tapped Horne's arm with her fan. "I believe you have some interest in the family?"

His face reddened. "Yes, that is so," he admitted.

"And I?" Prideau asked coldly.

"Have you written to your old secretary Hawks about Barry's letter breaking your betrothal?"

"And if I have not?"

She gave an impatient shake of her head. "Will you hear me?" The seriousness in her eyes belied the trilling laughter given for the sake of passing strollers.

"Patrick's life is in danger if no one comes to his aid. This bout of poison was a second attempt; someone cut through his saddle girth before a morning ride some time past," Glenna told the men.

Horne stiffened. "The broken arm?"

With a nod she continued, "At the time of that incident, and now again Pamela has fiercely accused Barry. I know the girl is of no few wits, but I sense a further hand in her words. And one that is dangerous."

"Who?" Horne demanded.

"Oh," Glenna frowned at him. "How can a simple widow know everything?"

"But you have a thought of whom it is?" Prideau said shrewdly. "What is it you would propose we do?"

"My attempts to dissuade Barry from departing have failed. They were off this morning."

"I shall ride after them now," Horne vowed.

"That will never do." Glenna fluttered her fan. "But Bath does grow thin of good company." She pouted. "I think it is a good time for a summer party in the country."

Prideau reading her intent, felt a sudden twinge of pity for Barry. "Does she suspect this?"

"Where are your wits, Prideau?" she said dryly, "I have been instructed to remain in Bath and fasten your interest; to rivet you secure."

"Are you, indeed?" He arched a brow, a slow smile spreading across his features.

Glenna laughed lightly. "What say you to meeting at Gromley Hall ten days from now?"

Prideau watched her with ill-concealed interest. "Is this party you are arranging for Barry—unknown to her—to be large or small?"

"Your cousin Lady Agatha would add a degree of—heaven forbid, propriety." She smiled. "And of course her two granddaughters who are here with her are to be included. You wouldn't know of two gentlemen who would welcome an invitation?" Glenna asked Horne. "We need our numbers to be even."

"With such a smile you could command the regiment," he laughed. "You need but to name the place."

"Why, Gromley Hall, as I said." She threw him a look of false surprise. "Did not your invitation read thus?"

Horne threw back his head and let loose an admiring laugh. He nodded to Prideau. "I see your meaning."

"Then be off," Glenna dismissed him lightly. "Ten days from now," she repeated.

Horne bid Prideau a good day, then took Glenna's hand and raised it to his lips. "I wish you safe journey." He smiled and sauntered away, leaving her gazing inquisitively at Prideau.

"Mrs. McDowell?" Looten's smooth voice preceded his elegant figure clothed in a fine jacket of claret-colored brocade. "How delightful to chance upon you. Prideau."

"An outing was necessary to cheer my heavy heart," Glenna said.

"Your company has left, then?"

"Yes." She sighed heavily. "How fortunate Lord Prideau and you still remain."

Looten assumed a crestfallen air. "I am sorry I must disappoint you. Only today word reached me that my presence is required at Looten Loft. Business matters are a nuisance." An elegant hand expertly unhooked his snuffbox; a pinch was carefully taken. "Good day." He nonchalantly strolled away.

"Barry fits Mr. Looten as a dandy," Glenna said contemptuously.

Prideau's gaze followed the man. "Or worse."

"Shame on you, my lord." She tapped his arm with her fan. "I have been justly cautioned against you.

"In truth," she continued with a sudden soberness, "I was astounded when I realized that Barry believes you responsible for Patrick's ills."

Anger flickered in his eyes. "That is a poor jest."

"And an equally bad one will see Barry to the gallows." Her humor was gone. "She has spoken nothing of it to me but I know her well. She is suddenly deathly frightened by the thought that you are seeking revenge. I recommend you write Mr. Hawks most sincerely. He will tell you who is in the wrong."

Seriousness fled as quickly as it came. "Ten days, my lord," she said brightly.

"If I am to be riveted, it will be best if I am by your side," Prideau offered lazily, deciding to go along with her plan.

"But of course." Glenna fluttered her long lashes. "How else is it to be done?"

Chapter Twelve

The morning sun shone warmly over the green landscape about Gromley Hall, drinking the last drops of dew. Laughter rose up to the windows of the sewing room, moving Barry to glance out. A smile lightened her pensive features at sight of the two lads dashing across the lawn towards the beech groove beyond.

Be content, she told herself. *See how Patrick improves.*

The lad's recovery had been as swift as the physician had foretold, but a foreboding still haunted her. Lord James was to call this morning and Barry had determined to broach his taking Patrick to his home.

Pamela strode into the sewing room, her riding crop still in hand. "I thought I could find you here."

"Did you enjoy your walk?" Barry asked, seeing that the hem of her skirts were wet.

The young woman's confidence was momentarily shaken. "Walk? I did but ride."

"You have become uncommonly fond of these early morning jaunts." Barry watched her closely, suspicious that so late a riser had so changed her habits.

Pamela glared at Barry.

"You wished something of me?" Barry ignored the stare.

"Yes." Haughtiness came to the fore. "We have been home but seven days and Patrick is himself again." Pamela drew off her gloves with an insolent glance.

Barry grew uneasy at her stepdaughter's tone. "I am heartily thankful for it."

"Are you, indeed? The concerned mother." The girl threw her crop and gloves aside.

"I would caution you to watch the sharpness of your tongue," Barry reprimanded with a sinking heart.

The sharpness increased Pamela's voice. "And I caution you."

"Your meaning?"

"You may have fooled the physician in Bath, and even Mrs. McDowell. But there are those who are not so blind to your scheme to have Gromley. Those who will support me if the need arises," Pamela said. "Patrick may not be convinced you are a danger to him, but we know the truth of the matter, do we not?"

Barry curbed the desire to slap the girl's arrogant face. "What you think will soon not matter," she answered calmly.

"The least hint that you mean to harm Patrick and I shall raise a cry that cannot be put down."

"You will not be given the opportunity."

Sudden fear entered Pamela's eyes. She stepped back.

Lord help me, she believes I would harm her, Barry thought and hurriedly said, "After I speak with Lord James this morning, I shall write to your aunt to inquire when she will be able to take you into her home."

"I will not abandon Patrick. You cannot make me," she said.

"Patrick will be going to Lord James."

"What?" This unforeseen possibility shocked her.

"Gromley Hall will be placed in the care of your father's land agent until Patrick comes of age. The details of an allowance for both of you will be discussed by Lord James and the barrister in London," Barry said, revealing her carefully thought-out plans.

"And you?" the young lady asked.

"I shall be taking a position as companion to Mrs. McDowell—or some other lady. You need not fear that it shall be nearby." A great tiredness sagged her shoulders.

Bereft of the response she had expected, Pamela experienced a singular sinking feeling. "You mean to abandon us just as Father did," she said hollowly.

"No, child." Compassion prompted Barry. "But I cannot continue to struggle with you. Whoever seeks to discredit me by harming Patrick may be persuaded to lay aside his designs if I go."

"I cannot believe you would go—"

"Then you have never truly loved," Barry said slowly. "Love does not ask for flattery or anything else. Love gives—no matter that nothing is given in return." She sensed the girl beginning to weaken.

"My lady, Lord James has come," her butler Tafte interrupted.

"Think on my actions, Pamela, and tell me honestly if I have done ill by your father or you." She laid a hand lightly on her arm. "We shall speak of this further," she said, turning to go to Lord James.

* * *

"My dear Lady Gromley." Lord James' speculative gaze turned to concern, his large steps bringing him quickly to her side. "Patrick does not look much harmed by the serious illness of which you wrote. But you, my dear, why your gown hangs upon you without need of lacings!"

"Bath society was hectic," Barry told him lightly. "Do you wish some tea?"

"Not this morning," he smiled.

"Please sit."

To her consternation Lord James drew his chair near hers and captured one of her hands with his large ones. "Why must I wait seven days to call on you?" came the gently disarming question as his clear grey eyes watched her closely.

There was a catch in her throat. How easy it would be to lay it all in his large, capable hands. "I wished to make certain of my thoughts," she began.

"Ah, my dear lady, I have also done so while you were gone." Lord James nodded, beaming.

"My lord—"

"Surely such formality is not necessary between us?"

"You are a dear friend but propriety—"

"I wish to be far more than friend, Lady Gromley. Surely you have read my thoughts, have known my intent?" The large man struggled to go down on one knee before her.

A deep blush burned Barry's face. "Truly, Lord James—"

"So that is your scheme," Pamela snapped, pausing in the salon's door. "And to think you near succeeded in your deception."

"Mind your tongue, young lady," Lord James said,

angered and embarrassed at having his proposal disturbed. "I will not permit you to use that tone."

"And what tone would you have me use to a murderess?" she demanded.

Lord James looked to Barry and back to Pamela. "You have had far too free a rein, but that does not excuse you," he told her coldly. "There is no way Lady Gromley could have cut the—"

"Oh, I do not speak of that. Has she not told you of poisoning Patrick?" Pamela enquired. "Are you her dupe?"

Anger stirred his affable mind. "What new maggot has taken hold of you? What is this of poison?"

"Lord James." Barry's features held a guilty cast. "When I wrote of Patrick's illness I neglected to tell you its cause. In truth, we learned it but a few days before our departure. I meant to tell you this morning."

"What else have you not told him?" Pamela asked. She turned to Lord James. "Do you know our lands in Essex and Kent are sold?"

"Of course," he answered nonplussed, scratching his head at this change in tack. "You cannot mean someone tried to kill the lad?" His gaze went to Barry.

Pamela recovered from his reply, throwing up her hands. "Someone? Can you not see what she is about? Gromley Hall will be hers when Patrick and I are gone."

"Enough," Lord James shouted, his glowering look intimidating Pamela into silence. "If I hear you spouting such nonsense again you shall have a birching, I promise you. To your chambers."

Wordlessly, Pamela whirled about and ran from them.

"It is my fault, Lord James," Barry said, her features pale.

"That young miss needs a tighter check rein," he said but his glare slowly diminished.

"But I am not the one to do it. She misreads everything I attempt and lately has thrown off all efforts to be guided. I wish your permission to write to her aunt in Chippenham to ask her to take Pamela."

He studied her keenly. "Would that be wise? Her ramblings—"

"She will have no call to mouth them." Barry clasped her hands tightly. "You see, I wish you to take Patrick into your home."

"Well, then," he said, beaming. "And I thought you were set on continuing alone. You have but to name the day, my dear."

Panic welled in Barry's heart as she realized how badly he had misread her words. "Oh, no," she blushed. "I did not—"

Glenna gave a slight cough at the door and then floated into the salon, her delicate hand extended. "Lord James, how delightful."

"Mrs. McDowell," the ample man greeted her cheerfully. "You are just in time to wish me well."

"Then it was a Derby-bound colt your mare presented you. How fortunate. I bid you well indeed, and hope to see it run," Glenna continued, sinking into a curtsy before him. She rose and went to Barry.

"I know I have arrived early, my dear. Do forgive me." She winked. "Bath was so dull without you. Ah, but I have interrupted you." She looked from one disconcerted face to the other's beaming smile. "No, do not say you were just asking after me?" Glenna drifted to Lord James. "Come, confess." Her lashes fluttered innocently.

"By Zeus, I promised to meet with my agent this morning," he spluttered under this feminine threat.

"Forgive me, Lady Gromley. I must see to it. We will talk more on this later."

"I understand," Barry answered. "But I fear Patrick may still be in danger."

"Only from himself like any other young jacka-napes," James laughed aside her concern. "You pay too great a heed to that young miss's nonsense. She probably ate a badly-cooled dish," he assured himself as much as her. "Write to the aunt if you still wish it." He shied from Glenna who had reached to lay a hand on his arm.

"But you will call this evening?" Barry asked, persistent.

"I—I may not be able to. Another obligation." He lied badly, nervous at Glenna's flirtatious pose.

"How unfortunate that would be," Glenna sighed regretfully.

"Yes." He attempted to bow, then bolted from the room.

"What a great, gentle Hercules." Glenna laughed lightly, meeting Barry's accusing mien. "Why such a pout, my dear? Did I not rescue you?"

Barry folded her arms in the pose of inquisitor. "I believe you had spoken of summering in Scotland. I have seen no heather here of late."

"Upon consideration of that scheme I became despondent." Glenna sighed, fluttering to the settee and sitting, her Italian lace gown a cloud of blue about her. "Indeed, it seems I mistook Lord James' words," she said mischievously. "Was there no colt?"

"Lord James mistook *my* meaning. I asked him to take Patrick into his home and he assumed *I* would come with the lad," Barry said.

"How like a man. But think how difficult it would be to convince him of his error. My dear, what a service you would do the poor man caring for his motherless brood." Glenna smiled generously. "For all his bulk, Lord James is uncommonly gentle."

"Yes." Barry paced to the fireplace. "That is why I have never been able to tell him bluntly to drop his suit. I gaze into his eyes, think of a hapless doe, and cannot send the shaft home."

"Come, surely you can draw a more apt simile. It is more the elephant among the cabbages I see."

Barry could not completely hide her smile. "Put aside your jests. I shall forgive you since you spared me a most embarrassing scene. I shall proceed with infinitely more care this evening. But now we must attend to the reason for your coming. I fear you shall find Gromley Hall exceedingly dull," she warned.

"Hardly, good friend. Summer parties can prove quite diverting. Do you not recall what an entertaining time was had the summer before my marriage?" Glenna settled comfortably on the settee, all innocence.

"Summer party? Then this shall be but a brief visit before you proceed to Scotland." Relief and yet sadness crossed Barry's tense features. "I might have guessed you were not so completely witless as to descend upon so poor an establishment without any warning." She smiled.

Glenna put on her best puzzled look. "Why, my invitation was signed in your name," she said, "if *not* in your hand." She winked.

A deep, sinking sensation hit Barry. "The Polduns," she moaned, blanching.

"How astute of you, dear Barry." Glenna's eyes sparkled.

"You did not—you could not have sent out invitations to Gromley Hall in my name?" she asked incredulous. Barry closed her eyes. What had seemed laughable when done to the Polduns so many years before now was not nearly so comic.

"If I recall, that party was a vast success," Glenna said soothingly. "I have ordered food, my house-keeper, and servants from my London house to Grom-ley, so do not worry. They shall begin arriving on the morrow, and the number of guests is ever so small," Glenna assured her. "Only six. Or eight, but then was it twelve?" She posed a finger on her chin. "No matter, we shall know their number in three days' time when they arrive."

Chapter Thirteen

Rooms closed since Gromley's death found their shutters thrown open, dust covers pulled from their furnishings, and quantities of beeswax applied to their floors and furnishings by hastily-hired maids.

Barry, far from bemoaning Glenna's mischief, found it a relief to have her mind taken from thoughts of Prideau during the day and to be so exhausted at night that her dreams were less disturbing.

Suspicious of Pamela's activities due to the last outburst, she forbade her to ride alone in the morning rides and insisted Patrick and Tabu go with her for any other outings.

The only real complication had proved to be Lord James' refusal to hear further on the need for Patrick leaving her care. He insisted Pamela's overactive imagination had colored a common illness, his past experience with physicians rendering a different opinion insignificant. Maintaining that the arrival of guests was just the thing needed to ensure the lad's safety if any threat did exist, he pronounced a blessing on Glenna's plans for a ball.

"Thence my doom," Barry muttered.

When pressed to the extent of the guest list, Glenna proved dexterous in avoiding conclusive responses, assuring Barry that no matter what its number she was certain everything would go well.

The appointed day came. A plaguing drizzle persisted past breakfast and there was yet another squabble with Pamela on the wisdom of remaining indoors.

Sitting at her desk, Barry was attending to last-minute details, checking over a multitude of lists when her thoughts wandered, as they too often did, to Prideau. She went back twelve years to the picnic they had taken with Glenna and Mr. McDowell. She remembered how they had left she and Prideau alone. She recalled how he had been half lying on the blanket, leaning on his elbow.

"I am still hungry," Prideau teased, eyeing her lovingly.

Sitting beside him, Barry daringly dangled a grape above his mouth. He opened it and she dropped in the grape. A blush stole up her cheeks.

Sitting up, Prideau reached into the basket and took a clump of grapes. He pulled two free. "Open," he ordered. When Barry did so he placed the grapes in her mouth, trailing his fingers lightly across her bottom lip.

Warmth coursed through Barry at his touch. Unknowingly she leaned toward him.

"Barry," he whispered, his hand against her cheek. "I do love you. I shall write every day. Shall you?"

"Never so much as I love you," she answered. "And yes, I shall.

They kissed, then embraced, her head resting contentedly on his shoulder.

Barry listened to the thudding of his heart and knew her own echoed it. She drew back, sighing.

"What is it?" Prideau asked, concern filling his eyes.

"Nothing," Barry said, lowering her gaze.

Prideau took her right hand in both of his. "Whatever troubles you can never be 'nothing' to me."

She raised starry eyes to his, her heart overflowing with love.

"Never forget that I will always love you," Prideau said slowly leaning forward, and then he kissed her.

Tafte's cough for attention startled Barry into the present. She dropped the sheaf of papers in her hand.

"Pardon me, my lady." He bent to help her retrieve them. "Mr. Looten has called."

"Is he one of my—" Barry halted. One could not ask one's butler if the gentleman had been invited to her summer party.

"He is in the second parlor, my lady." He handed her the papers.

"Ask Mrs. McDowell to join us there," she instructed, shuffling the parchment leaves into a neat stack.

"Good morning, Mr. Looten."

"The same to you, my lady." He made an elegant bow. "I was summoned to the Loft shortly after your departure from Bath. Only now have I been able to steal a few moments to give you my respects."

His smile brought to mind the stable cat toying with a mouse. She shrugged the thought aside, motioning for him to take a seat. "I would wish you a better day."

"How fares Lord Patrick?" he asked.

"Very well, thank you. He is almost completely recovered."

"That is excellent news. It is pleasing to see you also in good looks," Looten said. "And Miss Gromley?"

A swish of satin at the parlor door caused him to turn. The surprise and displeasure that skipped across his features confirmed Barry's suspicion that he was not among her guests. Looten quickly recovered and raised Glenna's hand to his lips before leading her to the sofa. "Such a pleasant surprise, Mrs. McDowell. How fortunate for Lady Gromley. But is this not an uncommonly dull place for you?"

Glenna fluttered her fan languidly. "There is much to entertain me."

"Lady Gromley, no insult was intended," the gentleman said.

"None was taken," Barry said, suppressing her increasing irritation at the man's condescending manner. "We mean to have a summer party. A small one, of course."

Pamela entered the parlor dressed in her best satin gown. "Mr. Looten, I had no idea you were to come." She blushed.

"You are very prettily dressed this morning." Glenna snapped her fan shut. "Ready so soon for our guests?"

Pamela threw her a startled look. "Indeed I am, Mrs. McDowell. The party was announced with so late a notice," her eyes went to Looten, "that I expect the guests to arrive without notice also. I do wish we had known sooner, Barry." She relaxed beneath the gentleman's almost imperceptible nod.

"You are in high looks, Miss Gromley." Looten motioned for her to take a seat on the sofa. "Shall your guests make a long stay of it?" he asked casually.

"How can one know?" Glenna gave a delicate

shrug. "If they are led by whims as I, no one may know the answer." She smilingly inspected the painting on the folds of her fan.

"Will your business require a lengthy stay in the country?" Barry asked politely.

"That is also uncertain. It may, perhaps, be for the entire summer."

"Since you live so close, Mr. Looten, perhaps you would care to take part in our festivities." Pamela glanced at her stepmother.

"Of course," Barry agreed after a brief pause, uneasy at the girl's maneuvering and Glenna's frown. "There is a supper tomorrow evening."

"And our ball is but five days from now," Pamela added.

"It is not so grand as to be aptly termed a ball," Barry said. "But there shall be dancing. You are most welcome to come."

"Then I shall count myself fortunate, indeed," Mr. Looten nodded.

"My lady," the butler entered the parlor, deep laughter sounding close behind him. "Lieutenant Horne, Lieutenant Stanson, and Mr. Lamp."

Horne, the first to enter, bowed to Barry and introduced his friends. The tall, blond, well-formed Stanson was amply complimented by the shorter, darker Lamp.

"Horne would have let us make ourselves presentable," Mr. Lamp said in apology for their mud-spattered breeches and top boots, his damp curled locks adding to his charm. "But so generous was his praise, that we had to meet Miss Gromley immediately." He smiled warmly at Pamela. "And I see it is most deserved."

An attractive blush rose to the young lady's cheeks

at this copious compliment. She glanced at Horne, then quickly lowered her eyes.

Looten approached Barry. "I regret I must take my leave. So kind of you to invite me for tomorrow. Shall five o'clock suit?"

"Very well, sir," she answered, holding out her hand.

"Until then." He raised it to his lips, his eyes flickering to Pamela as he straightened. "It appears Miss Gromley shall be vastly entertained," he said, his lips tightening. "And Mrs. McDowell's presence ensures your guests of an enjoyable stay." With a slight flourish he withdrew.

Glenna had joined the lively chatter of the four young people with her usual zest. Seeing Barry's signal when Looten's left, she ignored it.

His gaze falling on their silent hostess, Horne made an effort to draw her into the conversation. She answered his sally cheerfully, mentally thanking him for the opening she needed. "And now I must insist you gentlemen be off to your chambers. It would never do to have any of you take cold from your wet garments." She pulled the bell cord. "Tafte, see to the gentlemen. We take luncheon at one. Pamela, would you tell Cook there will be three more guests?"

Frowning at such a lowly task was prevented by the presence of the three gentlemen. "Of course." The young lady rose and walked from the parlor with them.

"And for you, *Mrs. McDowell*," Barry continued, "I think it is besides time we spoke of whom you invited."

"Certainly, my dear. You had but to ask." Glenna folded her fan carefully. "I have already mentioned Lord and Lady Black. Did I tell you their daughter, Miss Black, comes with them? The poor thing is a spinster, passingly pretty, but due a holiday from taking care of her brother's brood.

"Then there is Lady Agatha," she continued. "You met her at Bath? And her two granddaughters. Pamela will welcome their company; they are near her age." She named two more, then cocked a brow. "Does that answer?"

"Most admirably." Barry completed her mental pairings. "We shall sit to an even numbered table with Mr. Looten's aid. It was fortunate he happened to be in the country. Oh, dear, I've forgotten Patrick. He is to join us."

Glenna rose and moved towards the door. "I just now remembered that there is to be one other guest." She patted an unpowdered curl into place.

"Must I ask whom?"

"Oh, he is known to you—or should I say more aptly, was known." She pursed her lips.

Barry paled. "Say you did not invite him."

"Who, my dear?"

"You did not include Prideau."

"I could say I did not, but that would not halt his coming." She laughed. "I encountered him just as the idea of a party burst into bloom. Besides, how am I to fix my interest with him if he is not here?"

A ray of sunshine pierced the gloom outside the parlor window, bespeaking the end of rain and promising a beautiful English afternoon. For Barry the gloom grew deeper. Glenna could not know she was aiding Prideau in his attempt to gain revenge.

As the afternoon cleared, Prideau rode through the luxuriantly green Cotswolds near Gromley Hall. His meeting with Horne and his friends last evening had proved satisfactory; the measures he wished them to use in safeguarding Lord Patrick were quickly agreed upon. With this done, he had no excuse for going to Gromley Hall, and still, he was riding ever nearer.

If Barry allies herself with a man like Looten, she is all I have thought her to be. Prideau tried to comfort himself with the thought, but found it unbelievable. *The messenger I sent to London will soon bring the truth about Looten—and an answer from my old secretary Hawks about Barry's last letter. What had Glenna meant? What did she know?*

Turn back now, he told himself. *What ending could this have but more pain?*

Splashing and boyish laughter interrupted Prideau's thoughts. He reined his stallion to a halt.

"Patrick!" a voice shouted beyond the tree-lined river before him. Another splash sounded.

Prideau frowned. He should have realized he was on the Gromley land. A horse's nicker to his right was followed by a second from the opposite direction. *Likely one of the boys' mounts has strayed*, he thought, still debating turning back.

A glint of sun against metal in the nearby brush dispelled that thought. Prideau dismounted and loosened his sword in its scabbard. After fastening his mount's reins, he crept forward. He had taken only a few steps when his steed, startled by a rabbit, snorted and stamped nervously.

Snapping twigs, the dull thud of hooves sounded a hasty retreat from the position of the metallic gleam. Prideau swore softly to himself, realizing it would do little good to attempt a chase in unknown territory. Certain it was a fowling piece he has seen in the bushes, he was loathe to leave the lads, and so led his mount to the riverbank.

"I bid you good day, Lord Patrick," Prideau called over the boys' chatter.

Patrick turned to face him and was immediately swept underwater. Grinning widely, Tabu surfaced and gurgled with laughter when his master spluttered to the surface.

Patrick shook his head, then saluted Prideau. "I bid you welcome to Gromley." He swam to the shore.

"Then perhaps you will be kind enough to direct me to the Hall. It is almost time to dress for supper and I have lost my way."

"If supper is near, we had better hurry." Patrick said, climbing from the river, unembarrassed despite his natural state. Scampering to his clothing, he toweled dry with his shirt, Tabu following suit. Both lads made quick work of it, snaking into their breeches and tugging their boots into place.

"We can show you the shortest route," Patrick told Prideau, pulling on his damp shirt. "But we cannot go to the door with you, for you need to approach the front entrance while ours will be somewhat—different. Patrick frowned at Tabu's chuckle.

"The need to check a poulticed fetlock in the stables, no doubt," Prideau said gravely. He swung lithely into the saddle. "It is early days to be in the river," he commented quietly as they rode along.

"Only Pamela knows we do come here," Patrick admitted. "Barry would fly into a panic if she learned of it."

Prideau hid his smile. "Women are not understanding at times."

"Exactly." Prideau's wiseness impressed the young lad. He cocked his head inquiringly. "You are here for the summer party? I thought you held my stepmother in some distaste," Patrick stated with youthful bluntness.

"Quite so," Prideau returned honestly.

"Then why come?" Patrick asked, puzzled.

"A question I've asked myself often these few days past," Prideau answered. "No answer as yet prevails."

"Strange, my lord."

"Admittedly." He grinned and Patrick burst into laughter.

"Barry says if a man answers you honestly even when it makes him a fool, he is an honorable man." Patrick grew serious. "Are you such?"

"It is my hope."

"Then may I have your word of honor you will do nothing to distress Barry during your stay?"

Prideau studied Patrick closely. "Well spoken." He solemnly offered his hand.

"You would do well to ignore my sister's prattle," Patrick said after a few minutes.

Prideau arched a brow.

"Pamela is harmless for the most part, but she has this crazy notion Barry means to feather her bonnet at my expense, so to speak." He rushed his words. "Truth be known, Barry is far too kind-hearted for such a deed or she'd have slapped a tight rein on Pamela when she first came to Gromley," the lad confided. "Didn't you find her so? When you knew her ages ago," he added when Prideau appeared puzzled.

"Ah, yes. Ages ago," he smiled wanly.

Chapter Fourteen

Rising early in the morning, Barry hastened to the kitchen and found the cook and the housekeeper already in conference.

"A fair morning, my lady," the cook greeted her. "It is like former times." She motioned happily to the bustle in her kitchen. "The menus will be just as you ordered."

"Excellent. Are there sufficient strawberries for the tarts this evening?"

"Yes, my lady. All will go well, you needn't fret," she assured her.

"I suppose most of the guests will rise late this morning," Barry said, hoping to learn who was up.

"The three young gentlemen and Lord Prideau have already breakfasted and gone riding," the housekeeper informed her.

Barry's heart lurched. "And Lord Patrick?"

"Still sleeping, my lady." She glanced at the housekeeper, alarmed by Lady Gromley's intensity.

"And Tabu?"

"Also asleep."

"Have him come to me when he wakes. I shall

139

breakfast now. When I have finished we shall see to the flowers for this evening."

"Rest easy, my lady. Nothing will go amiss," the cook said trying to ease her mistress's concern.

"Yes, of course," she agreed. But it was not the food or comforts of Gromley Hall that concerned her.

Prideau was striding from the stables towards the main hall when a king bird's repeated call drew his attention. Looking to the park and garden on the east side of the Hall he saw the bird dive towards a figure atop a tall box reaching up into a tree. Recognizing Barry, he walked closer to see what she did.

"Please, stop that dreadful racket," Barry chided the king bird. She stretched on her toes to lift the paper sling in her hand high enough to deposit the baby bird she had discovered on the ground back into the nest.

Standing back slightly, Prideau gazed at her shapely ankles and allowed his eyes to meander past her trim waist and to her face, his thoughts going back to a summer party long ago.

"Drat you, do you not know I am trying to help your chick," Barry scolded the king bird as it dived at her again.

"Perhaps I can be of assistance?" Prideau offered.

Startled, Barry almost dumped the fledging bird from the paper sling she had devised from a list she had found in her apron. She gazed down at Prideau, her heart suddenly in her throat. Time stood still as she battled her emotions. They urged her to fall into his arms. Her color rose.

Prideau read something of her thoughts as he stepped to the box. "Let me help you down." He raised his hands to her waist.

Barry slowly lowered the parchment carrier and

placed her free hand on his shoulder. It was almost as if the years apart had disappeared. She wished they could stand like this forever. When he set her safely on the ground, she looked up. Their eyes met and she saw the years slide back, his doubt reappear.

Stepping back from her Prideau asked, "What were you trying to do?"

She held out the parchment with the tiny bird in it. "This fledgling had fallen out—I was hoping to put it back without touching it. You know it would never be accepted if I did."

Prideau looked inside the nest before taking hold the paper. "You always were too kind-hearted," he said with a reluctant smile. Putting a hand on the side of the wooden stand, he jumped upon it and then held out his hand for the sling.

Barry gave it to him. She watched as he stretched up and gently slid the bird back into its nest.

He jumped down and handed her the empty paper, his fingers lingering on hers. "It will only fall out again, you know."

"But I had to try—"

Under his gaze, words escaped Barry. The sound of pounding hooves bespoke the return of the others and both she and Prideau stepped back from one another. Without a word she turned and ran to the garden. Barry looked back as she picked up her basket of cut flowers. She saw him standing with his gaze fix upon her. Blinking back a tear, she hurried back to the house.

"Gentlemen, what are we to think?" Glenna flirted with the two young army officers, the first to arrive in the salon where the company was gathering before supper. "Are the Cotswolds more diverting than the company at Gromley?"

"Prideau may better answer that," Lieutenant Horne said jokingly.

Lieutenant Stanson smiled. "In beauty, you far surpass what I have seen thus far."

"Your commanding officers are to be congratulated," Glenna said, fluttering her fan. "You have learned evasive maneuvers well. But I shall not tease you. It appears your companion, Mr. Lamp, has learned his share of drills despite his lack of a red coat." Her fan indicated their friend entering the salon, a lovely smiling Miss Fairchance upon his arm.

"The devil take him," Stanson muttered.

"Gentlemen, it is but a minor skirmish and not one to win the battle," Glenna said.

"Mrs. McDowell," Stanson nodded, and, excusing himself, joined the trio.

Barry paused in the doorway. Seeing Lieutenant Horne with Glenna, she went to them. "Good evening, Glenna. Lieutenant Horne, did you enjoy your ride this morning?"

"Very much so," he answered, smiling. "You have cause to be proud of Gromley's environs." His eyes flitted towards the door. "Please excuse me, ladies." He bowed and joined Pamela.

"Have you learned why they were absent for so long?" Barry whispered to Glenna, but was forced to forgo an answer as two ladies approached. "Lady Black, Miss Black, good evening. I hope your chambers are satisfactory."

"Everything is quite pleasant, Lady Gromley. So restful and quiet," Lady Black answered, her nose giving a characteristic wriggle of approval while her daughter nodded quiet agreement.

Glenna took the plain-looking woman's arm, assessing what an application of cosmetics and a different-style gown would do for her. "Are you enjoying yourself, Miss Black?"

She smiled timidly. "Very much so."

"I imagine it is a relief to be away from your nieces and nephews for a time," Glenna said.

"Oh, no. I must beg to differ." Miss Black's features brightened. "I am uncommonly fond of my brother's little ones. It is lonely without their chatter."

"Truly," Glenna said. "Ah, here is Lord James. I must introduce you, Miss Black." She guided the shy woman towards the unsuspecting man. "The poor fellow is a widower with a brood of six to mother."

"I trust you have kept my granddaughters amply chaperoned." Lady Agatha nodded to the ladies in greeting, her attention taken by the animated group of young people at one side of the salon.

"Glenna is very capable," Barry told the elderly woman.

Lady Agatha spread her fan carefully. "Mrs. McDowell continues to amaze me with her abounding talents. But see, my cousin comes. Lord Prideau," she waved her fan commandingly at him, "do join us."

"My pleasure, Lady Agatha." Prideau bowed before the women, greeting each.

"Good evening, everyone. I trust you have found everything to your satisfaction?" Barry asked.

The sudden glint of laughter in Prideau's eyes eased Barry's unease. "I thank you for your invitation," he told her, sharing a glance of sympathy. "Lord Patrick is not here?" He glanced about. "He spoke of sitting with us this evening."

Barry's gaze flashed to his, searching for hidden

meaning, but saw nothing save polite inquiry. It seemed he had forgotten their encounter. If only she could also.

"Ah, my lady," Mr. Looten said, approaching his hostess and bowed before he kissed her hand. He acknowledged Prideau with a casual nod.

"I believe you know Prideau's cousin, Lady Agatha, Mr. Looten. Lady Agatha, Alfred Looten, a neighbor whose estates border Gromley," Barry made the introductions. "Please excuse us while I introduce Mr. Looten to my other guests."

Having introduced everyone, Barry was pleased to see all in agreeable conversation. She was amazed to see Prideau riveted to Lady Agatha's side, even more so to note Glenna fanning an evidently slow beginning between Lord James and Miss Black. The open-case clock on the mantel chimed, telling Barry supper would soon be announced. *Where could Patrick be?* she wondered.

Patrick's voice sounded as if in answer. "Lord Prideau."

He headed for him without breaking stride upon entering the salon. "It was poor sport of you not to await me for this morning's ride," he said.

"Tomorrow morning I will remedy the fault. Perhaps you would like to try my stallion?" Prideau asked.

Barry hurried to them. "He would not."

Anger rushed to Patrick's face.

"Supper is served," Tafte announced at the center door.

The ladies having removed to the salon after supper, the gentlemen were left to their cigars. One of the guests offered a lengthy report on his latest experiments in cattle breeding. Another challenged one of the conclusions given and while they argued the point, Lord James leaned towards Prideau, seated to his right. "Glenna—Mrs. McDowell tells me you have known Barry since her youth."

Prideau took a sudden interest in the candy-striped swirl in his goblet's stem. "That is true."

"A good sort of woman she is. Very good with children." He bobbed his large head. "It is a trial to me how she insists on being 'independent.'"

"Oh, Patrick is a good lad—steady as one could wish but that sister of his is a bloody nuisance. At every mishap blaming Lady Gromley." Prideau's interest encouraged him to continue. "At least it will be at an end soon. I mean to announce our betrothal at the ball," Lord James said.

"You and Miss Gromley?" Prideau asked.

"Of course not, my good man. Lady Gromley," the Lord James replied. "She doesn't want to hear of it but it is best."

Prideau's eyes went to Patrick while he absorbed this news. Looten was speaking to him as he had several times before. "I think that the ladies may think we have abandoned them," he said, raising his voice as he smiled at those about the table.

"That would never do," Lord James agreed. "Shall we join them?" He looked to Patrick.

The young lad waved a hand. "If you must. Remember we ride in the morning."

Chairs were heavily pushed back; conversation grew general.

Walking quickly from the room, Prideau caught up with Looten. "I had no idea your lands adjoined Gromley Hall, Mr. Looten," he said to his reluctant companion outside of the dining room.

The Misses Fairchance seated at the pianoforte were soon surrounded by all but the oldest guests. Lord James was snared by Glenna despite his objections and found himself next to Miss Black whom, he thought, while giving his own bellow of the current verse, had a light, pleasing voice.

Feeling his eyes upon her, Miss Black smiled shyly; this country-bred gentleman was not unlike her own brother whom she greatly admired.

Glenna took Prideau's arm. "We are in need of a baritone."

"Mr. Looten," Pamela called gaily from the group. "Do join us."

"If you wish, Miss Gromley." He nodded curtly to Prideau and Glenna. Joining Pamela, he said, louder than necessary, "When commanded by one as lovely as you, a gentleman must obey."

The young lady blushed her pleasure, moving to make room for him at her side.

"It is a pretty speech he makes," Glenna observed, fluttering her lashes at Prideau. "Why is it that you never mouth such foolishness, my lord?"

He looked at her with mock gravity. "You do not need it."

"Let us sit aside." Glenna pointed to the sofa some distance from both the pianoforte and the cluster about his cousin Lady Agatha. "My feeble mind recalls that I am to fix your interest. It is difficult to do when a gentleman insists upon taking to the saddle all the day," she continued, sitting down.

"Time well spent, Glenna. I still worry about Lord Patrick." He bent his head to hers, maintaining a bantering expression despite his words. Prideau briefly related what had happened at the river and told of following the tracks.

"Was the effort of value?" Glenna asked.

"This evening I learned the name of the holdings they led to—Looten Loft."

"So you say, my lord." She looked at the gay singers about the pianoforte.

"Miss Gromley appears taken with the gentleman." Prideau motioned to the young lady gazing happily at Looten's figure. "Perhaps she is just being true to her kind."

Glancing sharply at him, Glenna shook her head.

The evening sped past for everyone but Barry. Between her concern over Pamela's open display of interest in Mr. Looten, the ache caused at sight of Glenna's success with Prideau as well as confusion at what she had seen in his eyes after he had placed the fledgling for her, she quite shredded her fine lawn kerchief.

"A charming group, is it not?" Lady Agatha said to Barry, running a practiced eye over the couples. "Miss Black seems to have a good impression upon Lord James." Lady Agatha fanned herself slowly. "One never knows about the whims of gentleman," she said. "Especially one with six children on his hands."

Looten sauntered from his place at the pianoforte to Lady Gromley. "My lady, it is growing late and I must take my leave."

Following him, Pamela said, "I shall see Mr. Looten to the entry hall."

"You are so kind," the gentleman told her. "It is the first time in many years since I have been to Gromley

Hall and your assistance in finding my way shall be greatly appreciated." He offered his arm.

The glint in her stepdaughter's eye warned of a scene if she was challenged. Seeing Glenna rise and move towards them, Barry decided a few moments with Looten would not prove harmful. "Do not be too long," she said. "Good evening, Mr. Looten. We shall look to see you Thursday evening."

"Your son has graciously invited me for the morrow," Looten replied.

"How delightful," Barry said faintly, uneasy at the look he cast Pamela.

Safely in the corridor, Looten kissed Pamela's hand, then slowly moved an arm about her waist.

"Can we not tell everyone?" she asked. "It would make an excellent announcement at the ball," Pamela added, thinking of all the excitement her secret betrothal would raise.

"But she would spare nothing to upset our plans," Looten said, drawing her to him. "We must tread carefully, my pet, to survive her schemes." His grip hardened. "For one eager to wed, you flirt too much with Lieutenant Horne."

"It is but to fool my stepmother. She would have me like him."

Hearing steps, Looten released his hold and began walking forward. "Do you know who has the chambers beside Patrick's?" he whispered urgently.

"I believe Lieutenant Horne and Mr. Lamp are on the left and Lieutenant Stanson is on the right," she answered, puzzled at her fiancée's questions about Patrick.

Looten raised her palm to his lips as Glenna looked on from a distance. "I bid you good evening, Miss Gromley. Until tomorrow."

Pamela watched him walk out of sight. She thought of Lieutenant Horne's kindness to her even when she did not deserve it. Lately it had not been so diverting to contemplate marriage to Looten. His manner disturbed her at times.

Lieutenant Horne, when she admitted to it, made her doubt the wisdom of this clandestine romance that had seemed so daring and appealing at first. Of late Looten had produced fear in her, not tender emotions. And she was puzzled that the greater part of their conversations when they were private were about Patrick.

Chapter Fifteen

Chafing under the strictures of being hostess, Barry found the next morning interminable. Only Pamela and Miss Black had proven early risers, and while their presence among the gentlemen during the ride was somewhat reassuring for Patrick's sake, Barry still fretted about not being able to watch over him herself. His inclination for Prideau's company had shown itself again at breakfast. She did not dare put aside her concerns about his intentions toward Patrick. It wasn't until Tafte announced the return of the riding party that she drew an easy breath.

"Barry," Patrick called out, checking his running strides at seeing the other ladies were also in the garden. "You must come." He tugged at her hand. "We are to have a shooting match when the other gentlemen finish with the fowling pieces, and Mr. Looten will not believe you are an excellent shot."

The ladies looked askance at their hostess.

"Shall we not watch the gentlemen's prowess?" Glenna piped up in the silence. "Barry, what a brave soul you are to even touch one of those ghastly fire-belching iron pieces. I would give much to be able to protect myself with one."

Barry's cheeks reddened, but she refused to be embarrassed at possessing so unladylike a talent. "My husband insisted I learn."

"Come," Patrick urged.

"Let us go," Glenna agreed, marshalling the ladies to follow.

In an open field not far from the Hall, tables had been set up with an array of firearms and fowling pieces laid upon them while the footmen arranged a row of empty bottles sixty feet from the gentlemen.

Amid exclamations of alarm from the ladies at the smoke and the bark of the weapons, the men took turns stepping to the mark. Soon all were eliminated but Prideau and Looten. Several more rounds increased the cloud of smoke hovering about the participants but they remained even.

"My lord. Sir," Lord James addressed the pair. "Would you not consider calling the match a draw? It is evident you are both excellent marksmen. We could prove to be at this all afternoon."

"It is an honor to be accorded with you," Looten told Prideau. "Perhaps pistols shall show who is superior."

Prideau nodded, swallowing his desire to cut the man's pompous manner.

Turning away momentarily, Looten whispered to his servant. When he finished with his man, he told Lord James, "How fortunate I chose to drive this morning. Otherwise I would not have my own guns with me."

Lord James nodded, wondering what part chance

had actually played, since it was Looten who had proposed the shooting match.

"Barry shall take the first shot," Patrick announced proudly. "I am open to wagers. The distance shall be the standard set for flintlocks."

"Perhaps the target should be brought forward," Looten said.

"Indeed no, sir." Barry straightened her shoulders. "It is not the finger that touches the trigger but the weapon which determines the distance." She frowned at her stepson who was surrounded by the other gentlemen. "Patrick, no wagering."

Looten bowed with a flourish. "My humble apologies, Lady Gromley. May I make amends by offering the use of my own pieces? You will find them well-balanced and with a trigger that demands but the lightest touch." He snapped his fingers and his servant appeared instantly with a wooden velvet-lined case containing a matched set of breech-loading dueling pistols.

Barry took in the silver mounted settings. "They are beautifully made."

Looten removed one, smiling at its feel, then handed it to Barry.

Cocking the weapon with an expert flick of her hand, Barry walked to the mark. All eyes remained on her as she took careful aim and pressed the trigger without flinching from the recoil. A cheer rose from the men at the direct hit, and the ladies joined with them.

"I believe that is sufficient demonstration on my part," Barry announced, returning the pistol to Looten's servant. "I leave the laurels to you, gentlemen." She gave a curtsy.

"Well said," Lord James said, leading the applause.

As the adulation died down, Looten said, "Lord Patrick, as host you need to go first."

"My pistol," Patrick demanded, then a gleam came to his eye. "Lord Prideau, may I use one of your Spanish pieces? I have heard they are of the truest bore."

"Gladly." Prideau nodded, motioning to the table where they lay in their case. Looten's satisfied leer did not go unnoticed by Prideau, who had also noticed Looten's servant near the pistol table while Barry was shooting.

As soon as consent was given, Looten snapped his fingers, sending his man scurrying for the firearms.

Catching Horne's eye, Prideau made a quick motion.

"May I?" Lieutenant Horne walked to Patrick's side and reached for the pistol that was being offered to him.

The lad eyed him belligerently but nodded.

The pistol was quickly and expertly examined. Lord James observed the actions before speaking. "Who saw to the loading of this piece?" he demanded.

"I, of course." Prideau's eyes narrowed.

"It would have blown the lad's head to London if he had fired it."

Gasps arose from the ladies. Barry, a crushing weight descending upon her faint hopes, felt her worst fears verified.

"I should like to speak with you later, my lord," Lord James told Prideau sternly.

He nodded. "And I with you."

Glenna fluttered into action. "Gentlemen you must be famished. A cold collation is being served in the garden. Such a delightful setting, don't you agree? I am certain our appetites will be quite satisfied. Come along," she said, expertly herding the party forward.

Barry took a firm hold on her stepson's arm preventing him from joining Prideau and Lord James. "We must accompany our guests," she said unyieldingly.

Spurred by Glenna's animated spirit and Prideau's complete nonchalance, the mood slowly grew relaxed.

"Ahem—a delightful woman, Mrs. McDowell—if you like that sort," Lord James said nervously.

Motioning Lieutenant Horne to join them, Prideau said, "Let us walk a little a field. It shall be as private as any chamber."

"As you will," Lord James answered, puzzling how best to handle the matter, well aware of Prideau's reputation in the colonies, let alone his title. He decided on directness. "This matter of the pistols would be of naught but for certain other irregularities of late. Thank God Horne had the foresight to check the weapon," Lord James began.

"His lordship himself signaled me to check them," Horne said quietly.

"It is not my suggestion that you yourself overloaded it, of course," Lord James added hurriedly.

"And not taken so," Prideau assured him. "If by 'irregularities' you mean the attempts on Lord Patrick's life, I agree. He is in danger." He halted. "The person wishing him dead grows desperate to try so bold an attempt."

"You think this deliberate?"

"Yes. When I arrived on Gromley lands—" Prideau began his tale of the interrupted attempt at the river.

"By Zeus," Lord James exclaimed when the telling was finished. "You think Looten is this scoundrel?"

"I could not offer that to a magistrate," Prideau told him. "I have only suspicions."

"The man must be questioned," Lord James insisted.

"That would merely put him on his guard. We must bide our time and watch carefully. He must not realize his actions are suspected," Prideau said calmly. "Lord Patrick is safe enough with the younger gentlemen watching over him."

In the gardens, good food and affable company brought back the festive air. Looten added to it by paying generous compliments to all the ladies, favoring none. When all rose to go for a stroll in the gardens, several of the ladies went indoors to fetch parasols or bonnets and he used the opportunity for a few moments alone with Pamela.

"My dear," he whispered urgently to her, "we dare wait no longer. We must wed if Patrick is to be saved."

Deep consideration had dampened Pamela's enthusiasm. "Surely that was an accident," she protested.

"Has Lady Gromley not managed to make anyone she wishes do her bidding?" he argued. "I could not endure seeing you crushed by your brother's death when our speedy action can save him."

"If I renewed my accusations, revealed her scheme to all present, then she would not dare further action," Pamela protested.

"Such an act could give us the time we need," Looten said pensively, inwardly triumphant. "An easy escape cannot be had until the evening of the ball." Her quivering lip, the fear in her eyes affirmed his victory. "It shall prove the perfect disguise for us, for everyone shall be too busy to miss us till we are long gone. Say you are for it, my love," he pleaded. "For our own happiness, as well as for your brother's life."

Pamela's lip jutted out stubbornly. "I must think."

"Of course, my dear," Looten replied.

"Miss Gromley." Lieutenant Horne joined them before Looten could say anything further. "Would you join me for a stroll?"

"I shall be happy to," she replied, relieved to escape her fiancé's intensity. She refused to meet his eyes, turning away from him instead.

"You are uncommonly pale," Horne said as they walked. "Has the nonsense about the pistol frightened you?"

"Nonsense?" Pamela's voice rose, drawing the attention of the other members of the party. "I pray you not to take it so lightly, sir. That was not the first attempt on my brother's life."

All conversation ceased. Questioning glances stole to Barry.

"Indeed, he was not safe even in Bath," Pamela continued, speaking to the guests at large.

Patrick stalked towards her threateningly. "Pamela."

"Surely there are those among you who will save him? Save us—from her," she said, pointing to her stepmother.

"You must excuse my sister." Patrick took her hand, forcibly lowering it. "She is very excitable. Please continue," he said to them.

"Do not be such a fool, Patrick," Pamela said.

"Come." Glenna's hand closed firmly about her arm. "You have said enough," she said in a low, curt voice. With Pamela between them she and Patrick moved towards the hall.

The ladies began the conversation once more, the gentlemen gallantly following their lead. Looten threw Pamela a knowing glance, shrugging meaningfully.

Wrenching free from her captors, the young woman

fled, certain there was now but one way to save her brother.

"Lord Prideau. Glenna," Barry greeted the pair in the gardens later that evening, desperation driving her to seek them out. "I must speak with you, my lord. In private."

"I shall see what mischief the young ladies and gentlemen have gotten into," Glenna said and walked away.

Silence hovered for a long moment as Prideau studied Barry's downcast face. He hated seeing her so upset and offered his arm, outwardly calm. "Would you care to walk?"

She nodded dumbly, laying her hand lightly upon it.

"We are not unknown to one another," Prideau said after a short space. "What would you say to me?" He searched her face, his heart trembling at her helpless look.

Barry halted, raised her eyes to his, her hand tightening on his arm. "My lord, I know not what has caused you to hold me in such disregard. Nor what has prompted you to seek such a horrible revenge on me through Patrick, but I beg of you," her voice broke, "spare my stepson."

Disbelief filled him. He had not permitted himself to believe what Glenna had told him of Barry's suspicions. "You truly believe I could harm the lad?"

"There is nothing else for me to think." She dropped her hand. "We are both different persons from the two who pledged their love so foolishly many years past." Barry paused, searching his features for a glimpse of hope. "From your own lips I have heard you swear revenge on me.

"It was you who sent the poisoned treats to Patrick, and this very day your pistol nearly completed the work." She blinked back her tears, swallowed them with difficulty.

Her pleading posture, her voice testified to her belief in what she said. This was not the cold, heartless woman his mind had imagined. "Barry." He reached for her but she shrank back. "I could not harm Patrick." Prideau stepped towards her until a tree halted her.

She is frightened at your touch. Here is your revenge. The thought left him coldly empty.

"Dear God," Prideau whispered, his heart thrusting aside the fetters so carefully woven by logic and pride. "I must have been mad."

His wild look frightened Barry. He lifted his hands to ward off her fear. He watched her struggle to scream.

"Oh, God, do not look at me so." Prideau's features contorted. He stepped closer and gathered her in his arms. Barry remained paralyzed at first, but then began to yield in his arms. "How could you believe I ever hated you?" His lips brushed her hair while he asked himself the same question. Relief and joy swept through him, washing the years of bitterness from his mind as he surrendered to the love he had so bitterly, so determinedly suppressed.

A sob escaped Barry.

"You must know I could not harm the lad." Prideau's voice was thick with emotion. He gently raised her chin till their eyes met. Searching her face, he saw beyond her fearful hope, beyond the barrier, read her love and tenderly kissed her.

Barry, distrusting her reaction to him, exploded into a writhing mass. "No." She broke free. "No." She gulped for air as if drowning. "I was fool enough to let my heart believe you once. I cannot allow myself to be deceived again." The back of her hand smeared the tears from her eyes. "Oh, Prideau." The words slipped past her lips unconsciously. "If it were I you wished to harm—but you shall never have Patrick. Never!" Sobbing, Barry turned, stumbling on her skirts. Wrenching free of Prideau's helping hand, she dashed away before his pleading look could rob her of all reason.

"Barry," Prideau called, striding after her.

"My lord." Tafte appeared before him. "A messenger has just arrived from London and begs audience with you."

"Blessed Satan," Prideau swore angrily, curbing his desire to thrust the hapless butler from his path.

"He awaits you in the small parlor, my lord," Tafte said nervously.

"All right," Prideau answered him curtly, striding forward angrily. By the time he arrived at the room he had partially regained his calm. "You have word for me?" Prideau greeted the dusty, bleary-eyed rider standing uneasily in the parlor.

"Two letters, my lord." The man drew a sealed leather pouch from beneath his shirt.

Prideau took it. "Go to the kitchens for food and drink. I shall speak with you later."

The messenger nodded, and left him.

Breaking the seal on the first missive from the pouch, Prideau studied it. It concerned Mr. Looten and revealed nothing that he had not expected.

The second letter, from his old secretary Hawke, he eyed for a long moment. Prideau broke the seal, his hands trembling. Still hesitant, not knowing which he feared most—being proven correct after surrendering to his heart or having been wrong all these years—his eyes refused to focus on the open parchment.

Scowling, he forced himself to read. Prideau's heart lurched. A soul-rending groan escaped him and the words wavered before his eyes. He sat and read it once again, skipping over the first half to concentrate on what Hawks had written at the end:

> *And so my lord this is my full confession in the matter of Lady Gromley's letters to you during your betrothal. Her missives were always burned unopened upon their arrival. I kept only one back so that a forger could copy her hand to write the missive in which the betrothal was broken. I am ashamed to say that I destroyed all your letters to her when you gave them to me to be posted.*
>
> *My time in this world is not long, my lord. I beg you to forgive me in this. It was done as your father ordered for your protection. It is my belief Lady Gromley has remained in ignorance of the fate of her letters these many years.*
> > *With deepest regret,*
> > *Your most humble servant*
> > *John Hawks*

Chapter Sixteen

Thursday morning arrived with a glorious splash of light, one of those rare English days of sun, yet pleasantly cool, only the lowest land brushed by dampening mist.

Tafte admitted Mr. Looten without comment as the gentleman had roamed Gromley Hall like any other guest the last three days. "They are in the breakfast room," he said in answer to an inquiry and returned to his duties, vastly increased with the ball this evening.

Looten drifted to the gardens, for Pamela had shown a penchant for being alone there of late. He was about to go on to the breakfast room when an angrily upraised voice reached him.

"Why must you simper after that Looten fellow? It is beyond proper manners. Can you not see what the man is?"

"You make it very easy to see he is a true gentleman," Pamela replied angrily. "May I remind, you Lieutenant Horne, that you have no right to note any of my actions?"

"I should rejoice in that," he answered. "Hanging

on Looten's arm, lapping up the drivel he mouths—
you have thrown over all common sense."

A sharp slap rang out.

"You are insulting, sir."

"To think I considered wedding you," Horne said
bitterly. "Lady Gromley would do well to take a rod
to you. Why do you refuse to see all she tries to do
for you?"

"You are—intolerable. Leave me," Pamela commanded shrilly.

"I have done my best to reason with you," Horne
snapped, his patience gone. "I will leave you to your
own mire."

Looten watched as Pamela ran to a nearby arbor and
collapsed upon the bench within, breaking into sobs.

Looten approached and sat beside her, drawing her
consolingly into his arms. " "My poor love. Is it not
as I said? No one will believe Lady Gromley a danger
until it is too late. There is only one safe haven for
Lord Patrick—the home we provide him."

Pamela straightened in his arms. Looking into his
eyes, she saw only compassion. His gentle tone lulled
her; his words soothed her with their perfect reason.
"You are right," she conceded at last. "You are the
only one who listens. I will do as you say."

"You shall never have cause to regret it, my love."
Looten slowly turned over the hand he held, kissing
her wrist. "Ready what you deem necessary for a few
days' travel. I have a friend who is a canon in Reading
who will perform the ceremony.

"Ah, my love, the day will be far too long," he
continued. "But come, dry your tears. I must go and
prepare for the journey." Looten watched while Pamela daubed at her eyes. "You must give no one cause
to suspect what we plan. Do not speak of my coming

this morning, lest it arouse suspicions," he cautioned her. "Until this evening." He rose.

Pamela brushed aside the murmurs of her conscience. *I am saving my brother, and no one could wish for a more gracious or handsome husband than Mr. Looten*, she assured herself. *Certainly he was more sensitive to my feelings than that arrogant, pompous brute of a lieutenant*, she consoled herself, and ran inside before second thoughts could spring back to life.

"Did you learn anything?" Looten curtly asked his groom upon returning to his carriage.

"Yes, sir. Lord Patrick and his black servant have managed to slip away from the others and have gone riding. No one knows of it."

"Good." Looten's eyes took on a malevolent gleam. "To the Three Birches," he ordered, naming a place near the common boundary shared by Gromley and the Loft.

When they arrived he spoke briefly to the two mounted men who awaited him. "If successful in taking the lads, do not return to the Loft. I shall contact you in London." He dismissed the pair and ordered his driver forward.

The rose-colored satin gown was carefully tugged into place and smoothed over the panniers, then carefully hooked at the back by the maid pressed into service by Barry. "Please tell Tafte to have Lord Patrick see me before he goes down," she told the young girl when the last button was looped.

She curtsied. "Yes, my lady."

"May I enter?" Glenna said, peeking around the door.

"You are just in time to position these for me." Barry held out the matching satin bows that were to be placed in her powdered coiffure.

Glenna floated to her in a cloud of silver silk. "Sit, my dear, and I shall attend."

"Did the green gown fit Miss Black?" Barry asked, wishing to avoid any mention of Prideau, knowing her control would surely snap if forced to speak of him.

"Handsomely so." Glenna beamed mischievously. "You will hardly recognize her. It was good of you to give it. But are you certain you wish to be rid of your 'beau?' "

"I wish her all good fortune with Lord James. They should suit well." Barry smiled.

"No regrets there?"

"It will be a relief not to fear his approach this evening," Barry said. "But how can you be so certain his interest has been fixed?"

"They spent all last evening comparing remedies and potions for childhood maladies. He would not even be tempted from her side for a horticulture lesson."

"It is a good beginning," Barry said, then frowned. "I wonder where Patrick could be. He has been absent most of the day." She fidgeted as she spoke.

"Be still. I have but one more bow to fasten. There." Glenna gave a final pat to Barry's delicately curled coif. "You would be in excellent looks if you but rid yourself of that scowl," she said.

A knock sounded and Tafte entered. "My lady, Lord Patrick is not in his chambers. The servants have not seen him or the black lad since this morning."

Glenna's hand tightened on her shoulder, calming her first burst of fear. "Send someone to the stables to inquire for them," she said. "I shall await the answer here."

"Very good, my lady." Tafte withdrew.

"Perhaps Patrick did not wish to don the finery necessary for the ball," her friend said hopefully.

Fear filled her. "Has Prideau been about the Hall all day?"

"Why do you ask? You do not still believe him responsible for the attempts on Patrick's life?" Glenna eyed her friend incredulously. "After he saved him at the shooting match?"

"It was Lieutenant Horne who did the saving," Barry replied.

"Do not be a fool. Anyone can tell you by the way Prideau has been scowling since his arrival that he loves you and knows not what to do about it."

Barry closed her eyes and put a hand to her forehead. "Glenna, go down. See to the guests. When Lord James arrives send him to the small parlor. I will join him there."

"My lady." Tafte was at the door once again. "The head groom has sent word that Lord Patrick and his lad took out mounts about mid-morning. They have not returned."

"Why was I not told this?" She rose. "Have the man brought to the small parlor." Weighted steps took her slowly to the parlor door. She acknowledged Lord James's greeting curtly, immediately launching into an explanation of Patrick's absence.

"Probably some boyish prank," Lord James tried to assure her. "I shall speak with Lieutenant Horne. The lad may have made mention of the day's plans."

"Surely you mean to do more than that," Barry said sharply.

Glenna entered and came to her side. "There is

nothing more to do," she said, having heard his last words. "It is past time to sit for supper. Your other guests shall be arriving soon."

"I cannot," Barry said,

"You must. Lord James?" Glenna appealed to him.

"Mrs. McDowell is right, Lady Gromley. We cannot raise an alarm until we are certain there is need of one. Besides, no search can begin until daylight." He shrugged. "It would only worsen matters after Pamela's hysterics to—"

"How can you be so heartless? I care not what is thought of me." Barry turned on both, overwrought by worry and sleepless nights.

"Calm yourself." Lord James spoke roughly. "Nothing but harm can come if you allow yourself to go into hysterics."

"But—" she appealed to the staunch pair before her.

"It is past time to dine," Glenna repeated gently. "Come."

Barry passed supper in a maze of faces, somehow coherent conversations, desperate prayers for Patrick and that she was wrong about Prideau, her heart still refusing to completely accept that he was responsible.

The receiving line after the meal was no less a torture. In her own turmoil, Barry did not notice Pamela's nervousness or unusual bursts of shaky laughter. Nor that Lord Patrick's absence was not questioned by the young lady.

Entering the ballroom as soon as the arrivals thinned, Barry quickly sought to capture a glimpse of Lord James and found him visiting animatedly with Miss Black.

Prideau halted before her, his look begging an audience. "My lady."

"Yes?" she asked sharply, refusing to look at him.

"I am to lead you in the first dance," Prideau said, using the excuse to keep her at his side. He offered his arm when the musicians struck the first cord of the minuet.

Forcing a grim smile, Barry laid her hand on his arm. "I had hoped my stepson would lead me," she said, rising from her curtsy at center floor.

"Lord Patrick shall yet lead you in many," Prideau replied gravely. "Barry, I wish to apologize for my behavior—"

"There is no need," Barry interrupted him coldly, her heart breaking at the sound of her name on his lips. Moving away in the line of the dance she gave him no further opportunity to speak and was claimed immediately by Lieutenant Horne for the next dance. The other gentlemen were equally diligent in speaking for her hand, and it was several dances before she was able to escape and renew her search for Lord James.

After going about the entire ballroom, Barry began checking the small chambers ranged next to it. The fourth revealed Lord James, his head bent close to Miss Black's.

"Pardon me," she said, far too upset to note their guilty start. "I must speak with you, my lord. You will excuse him for a brief time, Miss Black?" She took hold of Lord James' hand. "He will be but a moment.

When they entered the corridor, Barry demanded, "What have you learned about Patrick?"

"Lord Prideau assures me there is nothing to fear." He patted her hand, anxious to return to Miss Black.

"Prideau! And you believed him?"

"Honorable man, he is. Why shouldn't I? I must get back to Miss Black," he blustered. "You must relax, enjoy yourself." Lord James moved back to the door.

Barry blindly made her way back to the ballroom and bumped into a gentleman just outside its doors.

Prideau caught her hand. "Barry, I was looking for you. You must hear me—"

"All I wish to hear from you, is that you will return my stepson to me."

"Barry," he said, "you must believe—"

"Will you not free him?" She took his hand. "What must I do?"

A gentleman approached, bent upon claiming Barry but Prideau swept her into the dance himself.

Barry closed her eyes against Prideau's beseeching gaze, forced to decry bitterly that her heart could still be moved by him, could betray her love for Patrick. At the dance's end she looked at him imploringly, then fled haphazardly to the veranda outside the ballroom.

Glenna had observed the pair and saw that all was far from well. She excused herself from her latest partner and approached Prideau's glowering figure.

"She will not listen to me," Prideau said. "I deserve no better. All these wasted years—"

"With more before you if you are dolt enough to stand here doing nothing more than scowl." She tapped his arm sharply with her fan.

"It is no use—"

"Fiddle, my lord. You would face Montcalm's Indians but not a heartbroken woman?" Glenna said. She relented seeing the misery on his face. "Go to her."

Barry ran a short distance from the veranda into the soft shadow of the hanging lanterns' light. No tears coursed down her cheeks. A deep hollow dryness overwhelmed her. Reaching a large oak, she leaned against its hard comfort. A twig snapped nearby, causing her to start, but she saw no one. Giving a shaky laugh, Barry moved away from the tree. "I fear your imagination has grown ghastly out of proportion of late," Barry said aloud to quiet her jangling nerves.

Suddenly a rough hand clamped over her mouth, another grabbed her about the waist and began to drag her into the darkness. "Don't struggle and it'll go easier for you," a man's voice grated in her ear. "Didn't think you'd be so kind as to come our way." He laughed. "You look to be a pretty piece. Perhaps you can convince me not to kill you after all," he said dragging her further into the darkness.

Patrick is already dead. The thought numbed her, froze her reaction. *Patrick is dead!* The words screamed a second time in her mind. Barry began flailing her arms, kicking wildly, her teeth sinking into the man's hand as she exploded in hysterical vengeance. In her frenzy she barely realized his hand had gone to her throat, and was tightening unmercifully. She heard neither the cursing nor the sound of running feet. Unconscious, she was flung to the ground, her attacker fleeing at another's approach.

"Barry? Barry!" Prideau dropped to one knee, gathering her tenderly in his arms. "Thank God, she breathes!"

Rising, he picked up her unconscious form and strode towards another entrance, not seeing the blue-gowned young woman moving stealthily away from the Hall among the trees.

Chapter Seventeen

Looten had told Pamela that he had snatched her brother from harm and would keep him safely at the Loft until their marriage, so Pamela had readily accepted Barry's declaration that Patrick was "indisposed." When Barry and Prideau had taken the floor a second time, Looten nodded to Pamela, giving their pre-arranged signal. She nervously and quietly excused herself.

In a few moments Pamela had secured her bandbox and was creeping through the gardens at the rear of Gromley, it being far too dangerous to go past the front with the plethora of guests, grooms, and carriages. Hearing a struggle, she hid behind a tree. There were running steps and then Prideau's voice, but she waited until he passed her, a woman in his arms, before rushing to the rendezvous point set by Looten.

When a shuttered lantern revealed Looten's closed carriage, she halted, her instincts bidding her take heed. Pamela quietly edged closer, hoping to learn more of the situation from the three men conversing beside it.

"What do you mean, you left her?" Looten asked.

"Why did you not finish her there? I wanted both she and the lad dead this day."

"At least the boys have taken care of the lads," the other said. "Jemmy and Tom did not return—so it is done."

Pamela stiffened at these words and their dire meaning.

"Lord Patrick is then indeed 'indisposed' tonight." Looten chuckled wickedly, causing Pamela's blood to run cold. She gasped, clasping a hand to her lips too late to muffle it.

The three men straightened to attention.

"Pamela," Looten called out softly. "Is that you, my sweet? Come, all is ready."

Whirling about, she ran a few feet before tripping over a root. Letting loose a piercing scream, she tried to rise before they reached her. Moments later a hand stifled further cries. Others pulled the young woman roughly to her feet.

"Hold her tightly," Looten ordered, grabbing her hands. "Why, my love," he warned Pamela with sweetly edged steel in his tone. "Do you wish to join your brother?" He laughed at her fear. "No, we shall be wed, you and I, and you will never tell what you know."

Stepping away from her kicking feet, he cautioned, "Think carefully, my dear. It can be easily proved that you gave me all the information I needed. Without your help the deed would not have been done. To the carriage," he ordered, his malicious chuckle following her. "Gag her tightly and put her inside while I see if anyone heard her."

When Looten returned he found Pamela tightly bound and gagged and deposited in the coach. "Halt only to change teams," he ordered.

Joining Pamela, Looten grabbed her arm and pulled

her from the coach's floor. "Take a seat, my love." A savage thrust pushed her down on the bench. "Lady Gromley may have escaped me this night, but never fear, my little love. Thanks to you, she shall soon see the gallows. Who else could wish poor Lord Patrick dead?" He let loose a half chortle, bracing himself as the coach lurched forward.

Glenna rushed into the salon opening off the gardens. She stopped short when she saw Prideau bent over an unseen person on the sofa. "What is it? Why do you need hartshorne?"

"Quickly," Prideau commanded. He took the small bottle from her and stalked around the sofa on which he had placed Barry's unconscious form. Bending over her, he waved the hartshorne beneath her nose.

Glenna's eyes widened at the sight of the dirt-smudged gown and the red marks about Barry's throat. "What happened? Who—"

Prideau's look silenced her. A moan took her gaze to her friend.

Confusion reigned in Barry's thoughts with the return of consciousness. Forcing her eyes open, she saw two forms bending over her.

"Some water," Prideau ordered.

Glenna quickly poured a glass from the pitcher on the sideboard and brought it to him.

Raising Barry's head, he poured a trickle into her lips.

As she swallowed, Barry's vision finally cleared. "What? Where?" She twisted to see past Prideau. *The salon. They were still at Gromley.* Barry grasped at the thought. "Patrick. Have you killed him?" she moaned.

"What foolishness is this?" Glenna asked, leaning over the back of the sofa.

Prideau's grip tightened on her arm, bringing Barry's eyes back to his. "I came to find you. A man was dragging you into the woods. Do you remember that?"

She nodded dumbly.

"Do you know who it was?" His eyes held hers.

"No." She shook her head, certain it had not been Prideau. "He said something about having to kill me."

"Is Looten still in the ballroom?" Prideau asked, turning to Glenna. "Or Lieutenant Horne?"

"I have no idea." She raised her hands hopelessly. "I saw them both earlier in the evening but—"

"Go see if you can find either of them. I shall stay with Barry. Hurry."

The light tapping of Glenna's red-heeled shoes had long faded to silence before Barry dared to look at Prideau. The intensity of his gaze smote her, her heart leaped at what she saw.

"You do love me," he said softly.

A small tear trickled from the corner of her eye.

Prideau gently smoothed it away. "And yet you believe I have harmed Patrick."

Barry could not endure it. She turned her face from him.

Rising, Prideau went to the bell cord and gave it a fierce tug. When the butler entered he said, "Tafte, stay with your mistress until I return."

A few moments later Barry heard his footsteps return and heard him say gently, "Open your eyes."

She gasped at sight of the lad beside Prideau. "Patrick!"

"Did you think me ghost's fodder?" He kissed her cheek. "But for his lordship here I would be. The two rogues who intended to make short work of Tabu and I are under guard." He smiled. "It was bad of us not to tell you," the lad admitted, "but we didn't want to forewarn Looten."

Barry struggled to rise. She sat unsteadily. "Prideau, can you forgive—"

He hurried forward and sat beside her, pulling her into his arms and pressing her head gently to his shoulder. "Always."

"Ahem," Tafte cleared his throat, beckoning his young master to turn away.

Glenna's exclamation of delight upon returning to the salon drew Prideau back. "At last." She beamed at the starry-eyed couple. "And Patrick, dear boy. I knew you would be found safe."

"Looten?" Prideau questioned Horne who had followed Glenna into the salon.

"Nowhere to be found," Glenna answered for him.

Horne reddened. "Looten told me you wished to speak with me in your chamber. I have not been able to find him since."

"And Pamela?"

At the shake of his head Glenna spoke before Prideau could. "I know—return to the ballroom and search for her." Realizing the serious implications of both Looten and the young lady being gone, she said as she dashed away, "I shall also check her room."

"I would not have thought I could be fooled off so easily," Horne said.

Glenna returned a short time later, gasping for breath. "Some of her things have been taken from her room. The wardrobe was standing open and her bureau's drawers were askew."

"Looten? Are you certain?" Barry asked Prideau, leaning into his strength. "But why?"

"Gromley borders the Loft. Together they would make an estate worthy of a marquess," he answered her. "Looten is a gambler, his lands heavily mortgaged. I believe he thought to wed you and join the properties upon Patrick's death. When you did not prove as biddable as he liked, he determined on Pamela."

Horne's hand went to the hilt of his sword. "We must be after them."

Glenna heard the strains of a minuet. "But the ball?"

"You and Lord James shall manage it," Barry told her.

"But you cannot mean to go," Prideau and Glenna protested as one.

"I must. No real harm was done me," Barry assured them. She pulled away from Prideau and stood. "Tafte," she ordered, "fetch my cloak. Pamela will need me."

"Yes," Glenna nodded reluctantly. "I shall find Lord James. No one shall ever realize you are gone."

Barry stayed her stepson at the salon's door. "Patrick, you must assist Glenna. It is your duty," she answered his hurt look. She accepted Prideau's hand and followed his lead.

"God speed," Glenna called after them. "Well, Lord Patrick. The ball awaits."

Two pairs of the fastest steeds in the Gromley stable were put to a closed carriage while Barry impatiently watched. Disdaining a driver, Lieutenant Horne mounted the box, leaving Prideau and Barry the privacy of the coach. Having frightened the two men who tried to abduct Patrick into talking, they knew to take the Reading Road heading towards London.

Prideau clasped Barry's hand while one arm held

her close. Neither spoke, both realizing the present danger would have to be resolved before they could speak what was in their hearts.

At each halt the hostlers were closely questioned about a recently passed closed carriage. Halfway to Reading, Prideau joined Horne, spelling him at driving when he failed to convince him not to challenge Looten once they found him.

Dawn quietly pinked the horizon's edge when Prideau halted rented hacks before the second inn on the outskirts of Reading. "We rest here," he told Horne, jumping down. "We all have need of it."

Horne reluctantly nodded and followed him from the box. "I shall ask about Looten. You see to Lady Gromley."

"Keep your cloak tightly about you, Barry," Prideau told her as he opened the coach's door. He reached for her waist and set her on the ground.

Horne stalked back to the pair, his hand loosening the sword in its scabbard. "They are here."

"Easy," Prideau cautioned him. "Let us have Pamela safely away from him first. Take my lady's arm," he commanded, still hoping to avert tragedy.

"My lord," the innkeeper greeted Prideau, recognizing the cut of true "quality" dress. "How many chambers do you desire?"

"None," Prideau said. "I believe you have a man within one of your chambers whom I would speak with. A man with a young lady. He is above six feet and in ball dress."

"Yes, my lord. There is such a pair above," the innkeeper said cautiously.

Barry stepped forward. "She is my daughter and only six and ten years. Pray tell us which chamber," she said.

"It is the third on the right," said the man, jumping aside when the three dashed forward at his words. "Better fetch the magistrate," he told a young lad who had just staggered in under a load of firewood. "It is likely there'll be need." He looked up the stairs. "Lord save the furnishings."

"Wait," Prideau commanded outside the door. "Barry, let her see you first." He knocked. "The water you ordered, sir," he mumbled against the door.

"In fair time," Looten said, jerking open the door.

Behind him Pamela cowered on the bed. "Barry!" she cried, rising at the sight of her stepmother. Seeing the two men behind her, Looten staggered back.

"Barry!" Pamela shrieked again and flew to her stepmother's arms.

Prideau maneuvered the ladies through the door. "Out with both of you."

Looten drew his sword as this was done, the steel rasping a warning.

Pamela's eyes went fearfully to the closing door. "What shall they do?"

"Defend your honor, child," Barry told her, a sudden tiredness descending at the sound of boots being dropped to the floor within the chamber. She made a quick, guilty prayer of thanks—it was Lieutenant Horne who had worn boots, not Prideau—and tightened her hold about her stepdaughter.

"You mean one shall die?"

"I fear so."

"No!" Pamela screamed and lunged for the door.

Barry held her back. "Can you still not see Looten for what he is?" she demanded angrily.

"Yes." Tears coursed down the other's cheeks. "And it is I who should suffer, not Brian—Lieutenant

Horne. I will die if he is harmed because of my conceit."

"Hush, hush." Barry gathered her in her arms. "You must be as brave as he is."

An oath, then angry words sounded within. There was a blow, then silence.

Barry fought her fear. "Lieutenant Horne is fresh from war. He has the greater skill. Prideau will see it is fairly fought," she told Pamela. "Disturbing them could mean his death."

Inside the chamber, Looten lay on the floor, rubbing his chin and regaining his wits after the blow Prideau had dealt him. He was not too dazed to see he had incapacitated Horne with the lunge he had made while the young man was removing his coat.

Having stripped the coat from Horne's arm, Prideau hurriedly bound a pad to the wound.

Looten eased himself slowly from the floor, reaching for the sword Prideau had knocked from his hand.

"Prideau," Horne shouted the warning after catching sight of the movement.

His sword flashed from its scabbard, quivering to life. "My pleasure." He ducked Looten's jab. "This shall be for Barry," he told the man.

The two battled intensely, the clash of swords ringing angrily.

"But for you," Looten said as they met, a parry momentarily locking their swords, "Pamela would have been mine—and Gromley Hall."

Prideau's lip curled contemptuously, the force of his thrusts increased with no seeming effort.

Perspiration beaded on Looten's forehead. He began to parry less quickly. Desperation took hold of the man while the Earl remained calm, confident.

Looten thrust; Prideau whirled away. When his

sword went afoul in the curtains, Prideau allowed him to draw it free, his point raised.

The formal salute given once more, battle resumed. Boldly thrusting, Looten misjudged his mark; Prideau's thrust went through his guard and struck him. Looten staggered back, crumpled to the floor, a look of amazement on his face.

Pamela burst through the door, her eyes widening upon seeing Looten, blood slowly spreading on his sweat-dampened shirt. "Horne," she cried, blanching at sight of Horne, blood seeping through his partially bandaged shoulder. "No," she breathed, her hand reaching for him.

Barry glanced from Looten's body to Prideau, who stood at one side, sword still in hand. "Thank God."

Horne pushed the fear-stricken girl towards Barry. "Take Pamela to the coach."

Prideau nodded his agreement.

Shaking, her heart still pounding painfully at the danger endured, Barry took Pamela's cloak from the bed and put it about the girl's shoulders.

"Wait in the coach. We shall come soon," Prideau told her, touching her shoulder gently, grateful for her calmness. "Horne shall be fine," he said. "Go quickly."

Barry guided Pamela from the chamber, breathing prayerful thanks for this ending.

After they had waited for a time in the coach, Pamela reached for her stepmother's hand. "Can you forgive me for the spiteful fool I have been?" Tears ran down her cheeks.

"There is much I would do differently," Barry answered. "You have had a harsh lesson. A man's death to recall all your life. It is punishment enough." She sighed. "Change will not come easily. Not near so easy as you imagine at this moment." She returned the grip. "But, together, we shall manage," she said, hugging her reassuringly.

"I always said all Pamela needed was a touch of sweetness to be utterly charming," Glenna said while chatting with Barry several days after their return to Gromley Hall. "They do make a handsome pair." She gazed after Horne, leaning upon the young woman's arm as they walked in the gardens. "It has been a diverting summer."

"Diverting?" Barry raised a brow doubtfully.

"And when shall you be setting your wedding date?" she asked.

Barry looked away quickly. "There has been no talk of marriage."

"Not still that foolishness about those letters?" Glenna said.

"No. Prideau made no mention of them when he took his leave."

"When does the man return? I saw no need for him to hurry off to London."

"He had to attend to the matter of Looten's death, and he and Lord James had a long discussion about Gromley. There was mention of his speaking to his solicitor barrister while in London." Barry said, unwilling to admit to anyone how her heart decried Prideau's hasty departure with no word from him for the week past.

"Then he has to see about the maid my housekeeper hired in Bath," Barry continued. "He is certain she is the one who poisoned Patrick." She sighed.

"Men and business. They must always see to matters themselves. It was the same with Mr. McDowell," she assured her friend. "And here is Lord James come to call." A hand fluttered a greeting to the ponderous man's hesitant approach. Glenna said, "His lordship is near to bursting. You don't think he has taken to stays do you?"

Barry nudged her friend sharply. "Welcome, Lord James."

"Mrs. McDowell," he greeted her. He shifted before them nervously. "Lady Gromley, may I speak with you—privately?"

"Of course." Barry sighed, thinking she would yet be forced to be blunt with Lord James about his suit. "There is no one in the salon. All our guests have departed save Lieutenant Horne," she said. "Glenna, mayhap you should join them." She motioned to the young couple.

"Lady Gromley has *no* romance in her soul," Glenna told Lord James with a pretty pout. "I shall see if the love birds have nested, never fear." She fluttered away.

Lord James stood grimly before her. "Lady Gromley."

"Yes?" She was puzzled by his unusual stiff demeanor.

He slapped his leg angrily. "Best to the truth and be done with it." Lord James drew himself up sharply. "I wish to be released from our betrothal." He blushed deeply.

"Freed? Betrothal?" His fearful grimace added to her puzzlement.

"I realize this is a blunt wound, but I am convinced we would not suit," Lord James continued. "You have often said it was best that we be only friends," he added hopefully.

Barry finally understood. Not wishing to hurt his feelings, she managed a sad smile. "Consider our betrothal at an end." She clasped her hands, his look of joy prompting a suspicion. "Am I to wish another felicitations?"

Lord James reddened guiltily, then broke into a beaming smile. "But for you we would never have met." He lunged forward and began pumping Barry's hand. "The children took to Miss Black—Elise—at once. We wed in a month. Say you shall come," he pleaded.

"Of course I shall." She smiled happily. "I congratulate you on your good fortune."

"I knew you'd understand," Lord James told her. He hurriedly withdrew.

Glenna sauntered back into the salon. "What did the huge bear want?"

"Lord James wished to be freed from our betrothal," Barry said, trying to hide her smile. She rose. "He is to wed Miss Black in a month. My congratulations on your matchmaking." She smiled. "But what shall you do now?"

"The country has grown dull, my dear." Glenna leaned the tip of her fan against her chin. "I think I have misjudged Lord John's worth." Her eyes sparkled with mischief.

"Lady Gromley. Mrs. McDowell." Tafte interrupted their conversation. "The messenger who brought this said you alone, my lady, were to open it." He held out a long, slim box.

Barry accepted it. "Thank you." She turned to Glenna as he departed. "I wonder what—"

"Open it," Glenna urged her excitedly. "Are you not curious?"

"It is probably some memento of appreciation from one of my guests." Barry lifted the lid. Gazing down, her heart skipped a beat. The lid tumbled to the floor and she drew back the soft, damp ferns with a trembling hand. Within lay a red rose.

His words rang faintly over the years. *This pledge shall not be broken by neither time nor by distance.* Cradling the rose tenderly, she asked, "Did the messenger bring anything else?"

But Tafte and Glenna had disappeared.

A deep voice sounded at the door. "Only himself."

"Prideau." She leaped to her feet.

He walked slowly to her, his hands joining hers on the promise rose. "It has been a lifetime since the pledge was given," Prideau said, his voice filled with emotion. "Can you believe I mean it as sincerely today, no, ten times more, than I did long ago?"

Nodding, Barry placed her free hand over his.

He gripped it tightly. "You are even more beautiful this day," he said. Then, "Your letters were never deliv—"

She placed a finger on his lips. "Glenna told me a little. You may tell me all of it someday."

He bent his head to hers and they kissed.

Prideau then raised a finger and gently traced the line of her jaw. "When can we be wed?"

A sudden frown appeared on her face with practicality's return. "There are Pamela and Patrick to consider."

"Her aunt is to arrive on the morrow. She has agreed to keep both of them for a month," Prideau informed her with a smile.

"There is the matter of Pamela and Lieutenant Horne."

"They have just agreed to a year's courtship. Horne shall be free to call whenever he has time from his duty." His smile deepened. Mischief danced in his eyes. "You should be delivered from your confinement in time for their nuptials."

Barry arched a brow. "I am not yet breeding."

"I know." He kissed her forehead, the tip of her nose, then her lips. "I have come armed with a special license and Canon Portman, an old friend of the cleric bent. I mean to remedy all obstacles, my dear, dear Barry," he said kissing her again. Prideau drew back reluctantly. "Find a gown you think suitable for your wedding. We marry this evening."

"Shall this suit, my lord?" She teasingly motioned at her plain Watteau gown, her features radiant with joy.

"By God, it shall." Prideau drew her to him once again. "If we can but find a moment to send for the cleric."

Barry demonstrated her agreement by drawing his head to hers. Her eye caught a glimpse of the promise rose still in her hand above his shoulder. Their lips met, sweeping twelve years into the past, the promise fulfilled.